AT THE COURT'S MERCY

Also by
KaShamba Williams
Driven
Dymond in the Rough
Stiletto 101

Anthology:

Around the Way Girls 2
Girls From Da Hood 2

AT THE COURT'S MERCY

KASHAMBA WILLIAMS

www.urbanbooks.net

AT THE COURT'S MERCY

Urban Books
74 Andrews Avenue
Wheatley Heights, NY 11798

ISBN 1-893196-29-1

First Printing January 2006
Printed in the United States of America

10 9 8 7 6 5 4 3 2 1

Dedications

My angel above:

Robert J. Ross, Jr.
September 7, 1991 – January 30, 1992

Thank you for strengthening me to press on. For years I was lost.
I celebrate your life!

Lamotte S. Williams, Sr.
December 16, 1951 – April 17, 1975

Your son and grandkids never had a chance to know you in the
physical, but your spirit lives on, through them.
May you rest in peace, Snotty . . . we hear your father's cry.

To all the fathers that are still standing—don't give up!

Also, this is dedicated to the ones that counted me out!
Guess what, by the Grace of God, I'm still standing!

Acknowledgments

Every day I wake up, Lord, I thank You! You know my heart, and although I fall short, You continue to bless me. In return, I do my best to bless others.

To my husband, Lamotte; with each passing day your love and support keeps me balanced. We are a match made!

To my babies; may you be encouraged from my hard work, and in the future, follow my lead.

To my mother, Shelley J.; I see that permanent smile on your face!

To my brother, Kenyatta; stand tall, stand strong and acknowledge the mercy and grace of God.

To my cousin, Kashamba; memories of MJ will last a lifetime. Remember them, on those lonely days. I've been there and even though the tunnel is dark, there are brighter days ahead. Keep your faith and the memories alive. I love you.

Mom Nita and Aunt Alice—If both of you were here, the family would be in order! Fierce and feisty, neither of you settled for less. Nothing but the best for your family. I miss both you so much. You were the link that kept the family together. Who will step up to the plate and fill the void? For the Fosters, I can say . . . cousin Angie ☺.

Pop-Pop, Grandmom Portia, Dad, Dee, Leslie, Alexis, Toni, Bonita, Malik, Aunt Robin, Granddad, Kenny, Angie, Aunt Paulette, Kim, Steven, my stepdaughter Jasmine, my stepson Lamotte, Kendra, Rhythm, RIP Grandmom Florine.

Lois Moore, Teali, Brownsville, Hank, Bop, Nap, Aunt Tootie, Tuesday, Janice, Rhonda, Uncle Edward, Uncle David, Donald, Shontia, Cartilla, Tish, Ronnika, Kimyatta, Ms. Almethar, Uncle Mike, Aunt Ethel, Candy, Bob Gibbs—Keep ya head up! Carlton, Pete.

To all my nieces and nephews; Aunt Rae loves you!

To my dedicated editor, Joanie Smith; to say thank you is an understatement. You challenge and make me go inside my mind to put the best words on paper. Thank you for your dedication and patience! Your work and late nights of work don't go unnoticed.

To fellow Authors

I've encountered so many authors during many phases of my literary journey; some have proved to be true and others, not. Those that are real and not covered with plastic, I salute you! Hickson, Brandon McCalla, Al Saadiq Banks, K'Wan, Joseph Jones, Shahida Fennel, Leondre Prince—*Me and My Girls* see that *Bloody Money, Tommy Good*! Shannon Holmes, Treasure Blue, Mark Anthony, Denise Campbell—you were a silent inspiration, but since I put it out there, now you know ☺, Reginald Hall, Joylynn Jossel—one of the most underrated authors in Urban Literature—You get my vote! T.N. Baker, Tracy Brown, Nikki Turner—you have your moments, but you're all right with me, Eric Gray, Victor Martin, Jaeyel, Trustice, Shamora Renee, Azarel, Heather Covington, Cho Woods, Freda Hazard, Shawna Grundy, Jessica Tilles, Ralph Johnson, Nishawnda, Deborah Smith, Crystal Winslow, Thomas Long, Jihad, Alisha Yvonne, Vickie Stringer—thank you for helping me build my name in this industry.

Carl Weber—Thank you for keeping me with steady work to help provide for my family. When a rough period came, you encouraged me to smooth out the dirt and keep it moving. *Around*

The Way Girls 2 was a good look! Thomas Long, LaJill Hunt and I, held it down! *Girls from Da Hood 2*—teaming up with Nikki Turner and Joy, how could I go wrong? But what readers better watch out for—*Around the Way Girls 3*—you never know where Juicy Brown will pop up . . . Where Dem Dollars At? ☺

Precioustymes Entertainment Authors

Lenaise Meyeil—Learn to accept the positives and the negatives of this business. Don't let people get in your head. It'll contaminate you. Hate comes with the game—Learn to brush it off. Whatever you do—keep on shining and don't let the stilettos fool you! **Stiletto 101** in stores now!

Unique J. Shannon—you've been riding with me since the inception. Loyalty—there's never been a doubt. As a commander, you've accepted your position. Keep ya lines tight! **Hittin' Numbers** in stores now!

B.P. Love – To say you aren't driving me crazy is an understatement! But, I appreciate your talent, drive and determination to succeed in this business. When your time comes, I'm sure you will prove your worthiness in this business. **Latin Heat**—coming 2006.

Tony Trusell—a man that respects the craft of being an author. You're not afraid to test the waters. Your skill, very creative, exciting and humorous, will have readers waiting for your next book. **One Love 'til I Die**—coming 2006.

There are a few authors, but it's too early in the game to put you on blast! Get those manuscripts completed! ☺

To the Literary Heads

Precioustymes yahoo group, C2C Readers, Mejah Bookstore, my place away from home—Emlyn, Marilyn, Diane, Jewel and Carmen, thank you for making me feel welcomed. Ninth Street

Books, Borders Express, B&N's, Waldenbooks, Shrine of the Black Madonna, Darryl Harris, Source of Knowledge, Expressions, Urban Knowledge, Sepia & Sable, Truth, Tru Books, Karibu, Tiff & Zyaire—thank you for always thinking of me for events! A&B, Afrikan World, Hustle-man Masaamba in Queens, Crystal Gamble-Nolden, Liquorous, Bookman, Khalil, Malik, Yusef and many more.

Angie Henderson—Read In Color, Raw Sistazs Reviewers, Yasmine—APOOO, A Nu Twistaflavah, Forefront magazine, LIVE magazine, The Grits, Heather Covington—Disigold magazine, Amorous Sepia Readin' Sistahs, Ebony Expressions, Mahogany bookclub, Sister2Sister, Lloyd & Kevin— www.theblacklibrary.com, AALBC, Go On Girl, ARC, Amorous Sepia Reading Sistahs, Sistah Circle, Ebony Eyes, Between Friends and to all the other clubs that read any of my books— thank you!

Special Shouts

(302)—Delaware stand up! Wilmington—Leondrei told me I wasn't reppin' like I should—'cause he reps to the fullest! I have nothing *but* love for the home team . . . to bad I'm in route to North Carolina. Ya girl will still hold it down though!

A special shout out goes to the readers that participated in the Respect The Struggle documentary—Tiffany Elliott, Trayonne Green, Aaron Fye, Lay-Low, Lydia Hill, Kendria Pugh, Tasha (from Queens ☺), Professor Shuaib Meacham, Timijha McKinney, Lorna Downey, Jenisha Johnson, Swannie, Anthony Saddler, Gloria Chase, and Angela Lewis.

To all the females I've counseled in the community centers, detention centers, on the phone, email and in my home – much love to all of you! Armelvis Booker – to this day, I use tools that you equipped me with! It's a time and a season for everything. I thank God for the season; he blessed me to have you in my life! Cindy, Ella, Autumn, Devon Chambers, Carla Banks, Shenetta Giles, Mil, Martina Gibbs, Shana, Shay, Donza, Cheryl, Shawnika, Tammy, Nicole, Tiffany, Shawn, Dawn, Cabrella, Russell, Ada, Michelle, Kita, Charmaine, Helen, Terrance, Keisha, Jimae, Red, Ronnie &

Timmy, Ms. Francine, Buddha, Brian, Darren, Randy, Squirt, Rhonda, Renee, Chalary, Mrs. Lois, Ronnie, Gayle, Sheen, Karen, Dee-Dee, Shawn, Demar, Deartis, Shell, Bryon, Raven, Tronda, Nina, Farren, Lori, Theresa, Robyn, Will, Lill, Professor Hurdle, Detective Mayfield, Detective Chapman, Nakea, Christine, Gary, Medina, Melissa, Kiana, Will, Rob Berry, Keith & Keisha, Spoony, Doug, Larae, Troy Stevens, Saundra, Kitty, Melanie, Verna, Wink, Simone, Linda, Tina, Tracy, Tilla, Roslyn, Elgin (Keep ya head up!), Duvowel, Picture That Productions, Crystal—All God's Children, Ocj Graphix, Foster's, Williams', Carrington's, Redden's, Ross' Gibbs', Armstead's, Moore's, to everyone holding me down . . .

To anyone I missed, please accept my apology.

I'd love to hear your comments.
Visit me online at www.KaShambaWilliams.com
Or, email me at precioustymesent@aol.com.

Other books by KaShamba Williams:

Precioustymes Entertainment: *DRIVEN*
Triple Crown Publications: *Blinded, Grimey—The Sequel to Blinded*
Urban Books: *Around the Way Girls 2, Girls From Da Hood 2*

Platinum Teen Series: *Dymond in the Rough, The Ab-solute Truth, Best Kept Secret, and Runaway.*

DVD Documentaries: Respect The Struggle Series: Hip-Hop Fiction

Prologue

Some Shit on My Mind

Six months ago . . .

Nakea

I don't know why Nasir thought I'd fade out of the mothafuckin' picture so fast. He thought he'd get my son and ride off into the sunset with his fake-ass princess Farren—*that bitch*—afraid the fuck not! I hate both of them with every muscle that you can think of. Farren stole my life and Nasir allowed her to. For that, she'll be sorry she did. I'm going to make her life so miserable, she's going to be calling me, cryin' to take Nasir and Li'l Marv back. This time, the shit I'm going to carry them through is some unthought-of shit compared to the stunts I pulled before. This goes out to all my baby mamas holding it the fuck down! Fantasia could'na said it better, but I will uphold the song out in the streets. I'm that baby mama you never want to meet.

My teenage love, Sean, was released from the halfway house and we are ready to wreck some shit together. When my thirty days ended in the shelter, I was receiving the keys to my project, income-based apartment, as promised. My sister, Shonda, moved in with me, and so did Sean. All the feelings I had for him, had been poured into Nasir, and I had to find a way to take them back and give them to the rightful owner: Sean. Nasir had stolen my heart from him and I had to deal with the humiliating fact that I was just a temporary broad in his life. Boy, did that shit bruise my ego. It's cool though. I'ma show all you niggas out there how *not* to fuck with a chick on a temporary basis. You might end up in a fucked up position like those mothafuckas!

The Jump-Off

As I bend over in my magnificently sewn polyester nightie, exposing my hind side while watering my roses that my young boy, Nasir, sent me that I'd placed inside the engraved vase Big Marv purchased for me, I'm tasting the last bit of juices he left inside my mouth, and *how* tasty it is. With my bottom lip pulled inside of my mouth and my index finger tracing my deep berry painted lips to match my nightie, on my upper lip, I can still hear Big Marv's baritone voice talking dirty to me, *"Home wrecker, dick pleaser, deep cock, nasty tramp"* . . . and the one that made me especially cum minutes after he said it with his powerful voice . . . *"Slut for a nut."* Thinking about it is making me touch myself in my most sacred place. Mmmm . . . Big Marv can still take me to paradise even in his death. Sometimes I dream of his touch, feeling his manhood deep inside of me, penetrating me like he was alive and well. That's why I had to make his son Nasir, the closet replica of him) do me like his father used to, call me the same names and treat me like the slut I was for him.

You think I give a fuck about Loretta? That whore can go back on the "ho-stroll" for all I care. That's where Big Marv picked her up. Had Loretta never told him I straight disrespected her ass when she was pregnant with Nasir, Big Marv might not had ever given me that ass kickin' and cut me off like he did. I believe had he not cut me off, my son Quinton would also have the Bundy name. Yeah, that's right—paybacks are a mothafucka! I'm sorry that my son's old flame, Farren, had to get hurt in the process. It's not her I'm try'na destroy. My vendetta is against that kooky bitch Loretta! She should have known Lena wasn't a bitch to take lightly. Nasir is the only way I can keep my memories of Big Marv fresh and also, my only way to cut Loretta straight in the heart, like Freeze did the day he killed Big Marv. Too bad, Nasir had to be "Forever the Victim."

Loretta

If Big Marv were alive, he'd a fucked Nasir up ten times over for letting a woman come between our relationship. Marv was a dedicated believer of MOB— money over bitches! Shit, that's how it was with me. He didn't let me interfere with him getting money. There were only two things that did: his mother and his kids. Nasir is just like his father. There's no doubt in my mind about him loving his son, but you can't tell me he doesn't feel the same for Nakea. He looks into her eyes the same way his father did to me. I see that sparkle that he has for her. Farren is a fling to make her jealous. That whole court ordeal was just to piss Nakea off more. Big Marv was a spiteful Negro and so is his son. Although Sheena wasn't his, he accepted her as his. He was crazy over both of them, but he had a love for Nasir that no one could ever deny—made me jealous and envious. How could he love our child more than he did me? I gave him all of me and he slighted me of his love. Not only did he take it away by giving it to his son, he had the nerve to die on me, leaving me with scared thoughts of whether his love was true to me.

When I replay the tapes and think about all the women he cheated on me with, I have to ask, did he really love me? He had to! I was the only woman he genuinely supported. Was I really the only one? Or was it a figment of my imagination? There were so many that he cheated on me with; Marie, Lena, Donita, Mallie, and a list of those corner bitches. But I know in my heart Francine, my best friend and "so-called" sister from another mother, had Marv too. I'm tired of acting as if I don't know. Guilt is hidden behind kindness. Why else would she continue to stick by my family? True friendship doesn't exist. Women who portray that are boldface lying! You have to watch them closer than your casual friends. Nothing is ever what it seems with women. Especially those who say they're your best friend. That's a pile of horseshit!

Anyway, that love affair with Farren will be over in no time. I know the heart of my son. Like his father, he'll fuck up. Pussy is their weakness. Maybe I should say having more than one pussy to stick it in, is. Neither one of them is satisfied with one entrée—buffet style is their forte.

The way Big Marv betrayed me, will be the same way my son will betray Farren—*Mark my words!* And like me, Nakea will be the one shining in the end.

Oh yeah, and that big head boy Quinton that Lena said was Marv's; that was never proven. It wasn't confirmed by a blood test, so I don't believe it! So, for all I care, Nasir is his only real flesh and blood.

Okay, real story . . . I do admit that I have problems with my daughter Sheena. But she better recognize that I had problems with my mother coming up. Flossy wasn't always this content. She kept the fire lit. Shoot . . . she's not kiddin' me. I guess what goes around comes around, and in Sheena's case, it's her turn to go through it!

Farren

You know, I'm about tired of this bullshit! Nasir must take me for a fool. I've been watching his patterns. Okay, it takes courage to change. Particularly since change was never embedded in him. His background is blemished, but who doesn't go through bumps and bruises coming up? And yes, I can deal with the fact that his mother dislikes me. Why? I've yet to find out. And yes, I've been able to get over his drama with his baby mama, but what I won't tolerate is too much more crap! If this man is going out on me, behind my back with someone else, I swear it will be OVER! I won't put up with the cheating. Its bad enough he backtracked with Nakea. Who's to say it won't happen again? The bitty still calls and does little dumb shit to get under my skin. I know what though, Nasir better get his act together before he finds himself without me.

Sonya

When I said Nasir should've never stuck dick in me, I meant that shit! Who dis nigga think he is, King Ding-a-ling like Trick Daddy? His shit wasn't all that anyway. Well, his head game is. Yeah, he talked that "yaddy-ya" about me being a ho, a slut and all that shit, but he knows I will put his ass on blast! He got a mean tongue game. That's why his prissy chick is holding tight. She probably ain't neva had a man go down on her like that nigga can. Fuck her! She's got to know that her man ain't nothin' but a trick. I see right through that nigga, she can't? Who is he try'na impress by taking a job at a school? That shit is just a front. I know he still slangin' and I'ma prove it! Besides, I know he still wants me. Dat nigga still wears his eyes on this head!

AT THE COURT'S MERCY

Chapter One – Breathe

"Nasir, can you believe we've been together for almost a year?" Farren gleamed, resting against the white and pink lounge chair at the beach, trying to dodge the sun's glare. Nasir hadn't visited a beach since Grandmom Flossy and her friend took him and Sheena when they were seven and nine years old. This wasn't even his flavor. In fact, he didn't want to be there, but he didn't want to ruin it for Farren because she loved frequenting the beach in the summer months. It was her parents who owned the beach house. Each summer they'd rent it out and always freed up a few weeks for family to enjoy it as well. This was the first time Nasir and Farren stayed.

"It's been that long?" Nasir barely mumbled, trying to concentrate on his thoughts of what was going on back home.

"Yes, baby, and I have some great news!" Farren gloated, repositioning the colorful beach umbrella so the sun's glare was covered for their eyes to meet. Nasir patted Li'l Marv's behind to soothe him from fidgeting during his nap. He wanted to go inside, but Farren insisted upon being outside to enjoy the beach fun with all the other beach goers. Nasir's body temperature rose for every second they stayed out there. Not from the heat, but from his anger.

"Tell me when we get inside. It's hotta than a mothafucka out here. Li'l Marv is baking in this sun and so am I!" he said, using the heat as an excuse.

Farren handed him a bottle of spring water.

"Tell me what good this is?" He held up the water bottle. "It's like spittin' at the sun. This ain't gon' cool me down! Feel Li'l Marv's back," he suggested to her.

He was trying to please Farren by coming along, but really wanted to be back home handling matters. He'd used his connection in more than one way. Professor Hurdle's husband hooked him up with a job as a teacher's assistant at the Charter School, where he was currently the overseer.

Although he pleaded to Chauncey that he wanted out of the game, it was all a ploy to cut him out of the loop. Nasir had partnered with Chauncey's connect on the sly and put his boy Brian, who was now the "big man" on the block, down; knocking Chauncey down a few notches. Chauncey was unaware that Nasir was behind Brian's rise in the game, and had in his mind to make hustlin' a thing of the past for Brian. However, he knew something shifty was happening with Nasir and was going to use his sources to find out what it was. The tension was building and Nasir wanted to make sure his boy was on his toes out there. That's why he'd rather be home.

"All right, I'll meet you inside. Do you want me to get Li'l Marv?" Farren offered, brushing sand off of her two-piece red and white bikini. The black panther on her backside stretched out as she dusted off her thighs and buttocks. She had picked up some weight, so the bathing suit bottom damn near fit like a thong smothered in between her ass, showing her rounded brown cinnamon bottom.

"I got him," Nasir answered, leaving her behind to pull up the blankets. The sand was hot underneath his bare feet. He had a pair of flip-flops that Farren purchased for him, but he felt they were too punkish and left them inside. Now, he felt the need for them; his feet were burning up.

Li'l Marv maneuvered his head, trying to get comfortable underneath Nasir's neck and shoulder space. Nasir's muscle toned chest caused a few heads to double back with lustful stares. He'd let his side burns grow in and had them trimmed to perfection by his barber. Walking as a proud father, Nasir winked at a couple of females giving him the eye seconds too long. Even with Farren as his woman, he was still a big-time flirt, setting the women in a fit like his daddy did.

"Grandmom!" Nasir called out inside the vibrant two-bedroom beach home. Farren thought it would be an excellent idea to bring Mom Flossy along. She hadn't been out of the house other than to attend her doctor's visits. Besides, the beach house was handicap accessible, so she could enjoy her time just like anybody else.

"Right here, grandson," Mom Flossy replied. The voice that was once powerful and full of life, was shaken and weary from the stroke, making her speech impaired. Nasir rushed out to the patio and wheeled her inside to the central air, so she could cool off as well.

"It's too hot for you to be out there. Stay inside with the air, Grandmom. Haven't you heard about older people dying from heat strokes?"

His comment was a little unsettling for her as she replied, "Haven't you heard about all the young folk dying by the bullet?" Mom Flossy's health didn't stop her from talking slick with wisdom. Farren laughed along with Mom Flossy, who was now giving Nasir a clever beam. After placing Li'l Marv on the bed in the master bedroom, Farren went inside the bathroom to change. In the process, the telephone rang.

"I'll get it," Nasir said to them. "Hello."

"What time will you be droppin' Li'l Marv off to my house?" Nakea demandingly questioned. Nasir had given her the number for emergency purposes. From the court order, she was entitled to all contact information.

"Don't start that bullshit, Nakea. I told you he'd by there by 6:00 p.m. tomorrow. You don't have to keep checking on me, a'ight?"

"Your girl must be near. That's the only time you try to shine on me."

"Where is your man? Ain't he home or somethin'? Go check for *that* nigga!"

"Whateva!" Nakea responded and ended the call.

Farren walked back into the living room, guessing from the conversation that it was Nakea on the line.

"Who gave her the telephone number to my parents' beach house?"

Nasir knew this would eventually lead to an argument, as it did every time Nakea called, so he knew more questions were coming. Farren had become more agitated with the circumstances than he liked her to be. She accused him repeatedly of messing around on her with Nakea, which wasn't true. He was still jumpin' off with Lena. It wasn't as much, but he was still sticking that. He had Lena under strict rules since she tried to pull that stunt at Farren's apartment. He stopped dealings with her for three months; however, when Farren kept denying him some head, he chose to bring Lena back in the picture. This time, though, he laid down a foundation.

He would no longer meet Lena at her house; it was too risky. He got tired of her saying her son was home and she didn't want him to know about her affair with a younger man. With Nasir never meeting her son personally, he had no hint that it was Quinton. So instead of meeting at her house, they'd meet at a studio apartment that Nasir and Brian rented out for business purposes in secrecy from Farren. When he was ready to see Lena, he'd call her on his way there and she would meet him. No matter what time of the day, access was granted; he could get it. Yet he wasn't gassed on her; it was the sex that drew him to her.

Lena, for sure, was the freakiest woman he'd ever been with. She loved golden showers (hot piss streaming over the body), gave an amazing blowjob, took it in the ass and she also loved to be titty fucked. Lena was *nasty*. Whatever he wanted, she was willing to do.

For Lena, it started off as a vengeful thing, just to be vindictive against Loretta and to try him out to see if he was anything like his father. Then, as the affair continued, she became acidic to the fact that Nasir had no knowledge of her son's placement in his father's life. How could he not know about his only brother? Up until the time of his death, Marv took care of Lena and Quinton. However, the reality of being a bottom bitch was oh so clear to her, since the only people who knew about them were Marv, Stan and Mrs. Anna—to her knowledge.

"I gave her the number, Farren, who else would?" Nasir was tired of the speculations and comments being thrown in his face about Nakea.

"Damn! She has access like that?" Farren stood back with her right hand on her hip. "Don't she have scheduled visitation? How come you can't deal with her strictly adhering to that?"

"I'm not gon' argue with you about this again. I don' told you a hundred times, ain't nothin' extra going on between us. It's strictly about my son, okay! I gave her the number because she needs to have a way to get in contact with her son at all times, and *that's* adhering to the rules! Wouldn't you if you had a child?"

Farren was trapped inside the paradox of her thinking. Just minutes ago she was eager to share the news about her positive pregnancy test. Nasir wasn't aware that she had tried vigorously to get pregnant; stopping the use of birth control pills. When that didn't work, she went to see a fertility doctor to master when ovulation occurred for them to try and conceive. When he told her he wanted her to bear his next seed, she believed him and made it happen. Her challenge wasn't having sex, 'cause they fucked like rabbits. It was getting pregnant and staying pregnant.

In her previous relationship with Quinton, she found out that her uterus had trouble housing fetuses. This time would be different though, she'd be extra careful and less active—whatever it took to keep this baby—Nasir's baby, which meant, not getting all excited for her blood pressure to rise.

Trying to breathe easily, she walked outside to the balcony to relax the conflicting thoughts. Nasir followed her, taking a seat in the beige chaise lounge next to hers, coaxing her baby emotions, while stroking her ego as she did his when needed, and at the same time, getting his way.

"Baby, ain't no need to stress about this. All of this is yours." He smiled, gripping his joint.

"Nasir, that's not funny," she replied, fighting back her smile. All Farren wanted was to feel that she was the number one woman in his life other than Mom Flossy and his mother. It appeared that Nakea was getting preferential treatment, making Farren extremely jealous, and internally, she despised that Nakea had access to him like that.

"You know that's all that matters. All you want to know is if I'm giving her this good wood, that's all." He sparkled with unashamed confidence.

"Maybe. Maybe not. It might be something else that she's getting." She cut her eyes at him.

"Oh, you mean this thunder tongue." He teased making waves with it. "You want some of this, don't you?"

"I sure do," she agreed.

"Let's go then." He pulled her up.

They briskly passed Mom Flossy, toward the bedroom. As soon as Nasir began to undress, Farren placed the palms of her hands on his chest, with hope fading.

"Wait baby, we can't do this," she sadly expressed.

Startled, Nasir questioned, "Why not?"

"I need to share some news with you first." She sat on the edge of the bed unable to break away. Nasir stood in front of her rock hard, ready to get in some guts—awaiting her not halfway, but fully aroused.

"I know you're not on your period. You wouldn't be wearing those little ass thongs."

"Nasir, they're not thongs. They're bikini bottoms."

"I can't tell. Whatever though, come on, my shit is hard. I told you about dick teasing. I ain't into that shit."

"It's not that." She rubbed her legs trying to ease it out, staring in the direction of the bamboo ceiling fan, not knowing how Nasir would take what she had to tell

21

him. "I'm pregnant," she blurted out, hiding her excitement.

With his stroking hand going up and down on his member, he responded, "Word? But what does that have to do with me hittin' that right now?" He had a strong premonition that she was pregnant from the weight gain and the strange late night cravings, but he didn't want to ask her prematurely, so he waited. Now she was telling him; his suspicions were accurate. "Damn, I bet that thing is nice and juicy. Come on, finish undressing." He started kissing her neck and poking her in the side with his dick pulsating against her. She turned slightly in the opposite direction to avoid his advances, largely because she was sticking to doctor's orders.

"We can't, Nasir."

"And why the fuck not?" He wondered with insecurity, feeling led astray.

"Doctor's orders, that's why."

He didn't like the sound of that—*doctor's orders*—as his idealization of a sex session lessened. "What do you mean, doctor's orders?" his voice rose. The natural progression of his hard-on began to reverse as his penis became limp.

"I'm sorry, baby, but not until I have the Cerclage procedure. By sewing my cervix closed, it may correct my condition . . . well, at least help. I've learned that I have an incompetent cervix that prematurely dilates. However, the procedure is not a hundred percent. In fact, about fifty percent of women who have this procedure done will still miscarry. But I'm optimistic that I'll be one of the lucky ones. We won't be able to have sex until then, because I'm at extreme high risk of miscarrying—doctor's orders."

Shielding her body, she logically concluded that it wasn't going down. This baby was her safe haven with Nasir, like Li'l Marv was to Nakea. Anxiety of being with a man, guided by the fact that he loves his son, she knew he'd love their child too. At the same time, she didn't want to tell him that she had been spotting blood, and that she was really afraid if she didn't take it easy, she'd end up miscarrying again.

"Is your shit that weak that you need an operation to keep a baby up in there?"

"That's a fucked up, insensitive remark to make, Nasir," she said turning away; profoundly insulted at her susceptible time.

"I'm sorry. That was insensitive. When is the procedure taking place?" Affectionate, in a warm loving way, he tried to predict how long it would be before he could get some.

Farren sighed, "It was scheduled, but . . . not until three weeks from now."

"What! So what are we gonna do in the meantime?" He needed to know. All the time they'd been together, never once had he received some head or and anal sex from her. That was out of the question. How was she to please him now?

"I guess we'll have to wait." She shrugged before he implied other options.

"What the fuck you mean, wait? You better start exercising those lips!"

"No I'm not! I told you before I don't suck dick. You got me mixed up with those other women that do that shit."

Before thinking rationally, once more he responded with his macho side, "Yeah, I guess I do." Leaving her stuck with his words.

"Yeah, well, you can get them to do it for you, 'cause I'm not! And by the way, congrats on being a daddy again, since all you care about is bustin' a nut."

It wasn't that important. He was horny, that's all—watching her dimple free, smoothed-out tanned ass in that little ass two-piece bathing suit. He was ready to fuck after watching her ass jiggle, walking back to the house from the beach.

Frustrated, he pulled up his shorts from around his ankles and gridlocked on her. "I didn't mean that. I was just talking shit." Walking to the side of the bed where she was, he got down on his knees, stroking

24

her. "I guess you can't have none of this thick tickle either," he said, spreading open her legs while easing between them, drawing in desperation, believing that she would let her guard down.

"Nope!" she quickly reproached, closing her legs tight. "An orgasm could also make me miscarry."

His head dropped between her legs. "Then, baby, you have to please me some way. I'm a young man with needs. I can't go without."

"Best I can do is jerk you, but—" She twitched her upper lip. "Don't cum all on my hand and fingers. That's a nasty, gooey mess!"

Back At It

When the pimp tries to get at you—drop it likes it's hot, drop it likes it's hot. Shonda danced around the living room watching music videos with Nakea and Sean.

"Would you sit your funky ass down? You're in my way. I'm try'na check honey out that's droppin' that thang." Sean swatted in Shonda's direction. Sitting on a pillow on the floor, between Nakea's legs, he was getting his braids redone. Nakea's back was arched forward, skillfully parting his hair, applying grease in between before braiding.

"Shonda, move!" Nakea swatted with her man.

"Y'all, bitches, tag teaming me?" Shonda had become a nuisance around the house; always complaining about Sean and Nakea arguing. Agitatedly with that, and Nakea's dealings with Loretta, she tried everything she could to keep her sister from getting hurt. But it was Shonda's influence that kept Nakea doing foul shit to Farren. She had convinced her to bust out her car windows, slice her tires, key up her car, and when she saw that didn't work to provoke Farren to retaliate against them, they did the ultimate damage to her car—poured sugar in the tank. Farren's

26

old school Toyota Corolla shut right down. That finally made Farren respond, but still not in a manner they thought she should. They were heated when Farren pulled up two days later with a new Infinite G20. It was the norm for them to call Farren and curse her out; she was accustomed to that child's play. However, recently, their verbal threats to Farren made her more concerned, especially since she had a baby on the way. But Nakea and Shonda didn't know that, so it didn't matter. They continued to squabble as usual.

"What time is dat nigga droppin' off my nephew?" Shonda asked, pitfalls in between, referring to Nasir.

"His name is Nasir *and* he's still my baby daddy, *all right.*" Nakea felt that her and Nasir's relationship was getting better, but the order from family court was about to change. If she remained cordial to him, she thought he would agree with revising the court order. Never considering that her maltreatment of his woman, might make him remotely against her.

"You takin' up for that bitch-made mothafucka?" Sean interjected, already holding animosity against Nasir for taking his woman. Sean knew that Nakea still secretly had intimate feelings for him, but used scare tactics to make her forget.

As with Farren and Nasir, Nakea and Sean's verbal fights stemmed from the mention of either name; Nasir or Nakea. Sean took it a step further though; he'd mentally and physically abused Nakea several times over the reference of her baby daddy's name.

"She don't want him." Shonda jumped in before Sean started on her.

"Shut the fuck up! Nobody is talkin' to you."

Nakea finished his last braid, bending in his hang time (the excess braided hair that hangs on your neck. The coal black strands of hair blended with his charcoal complexion.

"You can start trippin' if you want nig-ga, but we'll bank yo' ass today!" Shonda stood there waiting for him to make a move. Sean's inner rage plunged his heart, causing him to slowly mangle his face muscles toward Nakea.

"Yo, if I find out you're so much as talking to dude, I'ma kill you, Nakea. My word is true—fuck wit' me if you want!"

Shonda undertook her big sister role and once more challenged Sean. "Ain't no damn body dying in this house unless it's you mothafucka, so you can stop with all the threats."

"But this ain't a threat . . ." He wanted both of them to let that sink in; Forcing them to think the worst. ". . . It's a promise!" Sean hurtled to the door, slamming it behind him. Resentment had grown over the months and was cancerous.

"See, that's why it was a bad decision for you to get back with him. You know a man can't take it when the next man comes around that's been hittin' his kitten." Shonda had once perceived Sean as *that dude*, but now wished that he would vanish out of her sister's life. In the long run, she felt Nakea was better off without him.

"That's all talk, Shonda. Sean would never do anything to hurt me." Nakea tried hard to convince herself of that.

"So beatin' ya ass ain't proof enough?"

"I provoke him most of the time. That's why we fight."

"Don't tell me you are one of those 'in denial' bitches! When a man threatens your life, you betta take it for what it's worth, gurl!"

Nakea needed an excuse to clear her man, becoming dispirited, listening to Shonda sabotage him. "It's funny how you pop off at the mouth about Sean or Nasir, when you don't have a man."

Shonda had to laugh at her sister soaking in self pity. "Whateva! Neither one of those niggas ain't shit. In case you forgot, Nasir dumped yo' ass, and Sean only got back with you to prove a point to dat nigga. His ego wouldn't allow him to sit back, thinking another man got his girl. And for the record, *I don't need a man*, especially if they act like yours!"

29

Nakea sat sideways and her eyes were red, as if she'd been smoking a little haze; however, it was from the salt, stinging the hell out of her pupils. It was the middle of the afternoon and both Shonda and Sean had clouded her mind with wickedness.

She picked up the fingernail polish remover to remove the chipped nail polish on her nails. Shonda fumbled around in the living room looking for nothing but a response from Nakea.

"I guess you mad now, huh?"

Nakea turned her cheek, pouting her lips. Yes, she was mad, and seconds shy of calling Shonda out on her trifling behaviors. Who was she to judge her?

"If you was a chicken on the street, I'd fuck you up. But you're my sister, so I'ma chill and let you say your peace. Only 'cause you got my back and I know you wouldn't intentionally try to hurt me," Nakea explained to her. Shonda came near, and quickly put Nakea in a headlock, causing her to drop the bottle of nail polish on her shorts.

"You can't beat me if you tried, Nakea, so don't try me, baby girl." She let loose, smiling back at her. "You betta watch dat nigga though. He's on a death mission." Nakea nodded her head and got up to change her clothes, without fussing at her for messing up her cute outfit.

This Is a Man's World

Outside on this hot summer day cooled by the constant breeze of humid air that brushed the trees, Sean's unrestrained anger had him ready to get his. All the moneymakers were out doing what they knew best—getting money.

Sean pulled up on Chauncey with his muscle-tight wife beater and a pair of blue State Property jean shorts, looking casually thugged out.

"What up, playboy?" Sean said giving Chauncey some dap. Sean was one of those get-rich-or-die-trying type of cats, so Chauncey knew what he was coming to approach him about: some work.

"Gettin' money, nigga. How's your cash flow? You on your feet yet?" Chauncey checked the resiliency that motivated him.

"My doe is low. Pretty soon a nigga might have to do what he gotta do to eat. I ain't gon' sit around watchin' niggas get theirs, while I'm starving. I'm ready to make some power moves. Can you help a nigga on the rise? I need some work!"

"Yo, you know I had mad dealings with your woman's ex, right?"

"Fuck that punk-ass nigga! He left her and his son out there. Nigga ain't shit! I don't care what type dealings you had with him. This is about me and gettin' cheddar!" Poison ran through his veins.

Chauncey smiled brightly on the inside, not showing Sean how pleased he was to see that he had no love for Nasir either. This ordained Sean was ready to join him in bringing Nasir down for bailing out on him. Ever since Nasir left him hanging, his product was moving slow, proving that Nasir was the one really making the money while Chauncey splurged carelessly with his take of it.

"That's what I'm screamin' too—fuck niggas that ain't try'na get money! But if you really serious." He looked from side to side. "I got a job for you to do to match your mouthpiece." Chauncey made a promise to never let his workers leave without holding baggage over their head. If they wanted out like Nasir, he would hold that shit against them; making them stay or at least move more packages to keep him ahead of the game.

When Nasir skipped on him, he had a brick and a half of cocaine to move solo. The rest of the Horsemen crew were hemmed up in an indictment and were each facing jail time. So was the person that ratted them out, and that left Chauncey, ass out. He couldn't tell his supplier that he was incapable of moving product because that would further decrease the amount of coke he received. So he hustled overtime and got the product sold. He did that—sold every gram he cooked up. But that caused a rage of fury that he aimed specifically at Nasir for putting him in that position, when he was the reason for his come up. No, he wasn't letting that shit happen to him again. Plus, Sean would serve two-fold: getting money and taking Nasir out.

"You know the boy B-Right that hang with the nigga that was pluckin' ya girl off?" He saw the devil horns growing from Sean's head.

"Yo, don't keep disrespecting me like that, man!"

Chauncey's hands went in the air, clearing any bad vibes that were forming. "You got that, bro, but do you know B?"

"I've seen him around. What about him?"

"He makin' major figures out here and he rolls solo too. You gotta piece?"

"Nah, I'm ass out since I came home. I know you have one I can strap."

"Yeah, yeah, meet me later on tonight at the corner of Martin Luther King Boulevard and Walnut, under the bridge, for your shit. I want you to hit the nigga up. Don't shoot him, just take the nigga for all his ends, and scare the mothafucka, that's all."

"Good as done. See you later on. One, nigga." Sean bopped away with his untied Timbs flopping sloppily off his feet, eagerly anticipating the sun setting. Chauncey nodded anxiously, knowing that shit was about to heat up.

❦❦❦❦❦

Nasir opened the door for Grandmom Flossy and was immediately greeted by Sheena, who was ready to assist him. Walking over to the car, she went to lift her grandmother out.

"Just grab the wheelchair. I got grandmom." Nasir began to lift Mom Flossy from the seat.

"I can get out on my own. You kids act like I'm helpless," she fussed.

Nasir had traded in the Mazda 929 for a white Lincoln Town Car with sparkling, spinning rims and tinted windows. He took the old playas back with the Lincoln Town Car symbol dangling from his rearview mirror.

Mom Flossy reached for the top handlebar to balance her precariousness. Beltless, Nasir kept using his hands to keep his pants up, while bending down to grip Mom Flossy underneath her underarms. Sheena had the wheelchair out and ready for her to plop down in.

"Hey, Farren," Sheena spoke. Little Marv was knocked out in the back seat and Farren wasn't too far behind him. They were all exhausted from the heat.

"Oh, hey, Sheena," Farren spoke back. Leslie, Farren's mother, told her never to get too involved in a man's family, unless he was the man she planned on marrying. Farren was sure that she loved Nasir, but was skeptical about bonding with his side of the family. And marriage—she didn't see transpiring anytime soon.

Mom Flossy could hear the phone ringing from the outside. "Hurry, now . . . that might be Joe the number man. I need to get my night numbers in!"

"Grandmom, we're not rushing so you can play the street numbers." Nasir had her in the wheelchair, leading her to the handicap ramp he had installed, that attached to the newly enclosed front porch.

"Yes, the hell you better! Shit, I might hit that 312 or 611 tonight. My palms been itchin'. I can see my money now!"

Sheena came to the door out of breath from running upstairs to answer the cordless. "Nasir, the phone's for you."

"Who is it?"

Sheena signaled him with her eyes trying to cover up for him. "Who else calls this line for you *but* bill collectors?"

"Next time, tell them I don't live here anymore." Nasir got the hint his sister threw.

Farren watched suspiciously as he took the phone. "Yeah?"

It was Lena asking, "Why won't you answer my calls?"

Nasir quickly threw Lena a bone. "Before taking me to collections, don't I at least receive a courtesy call?"

"I see . . . you're with her." The way Lena said *her* had to make her nose burn from an invigorating fragrance called envy.

"I'll tell you what, the best I can do is balance what little I have. If that's not good enough for you, don't call here anymore, because I'm limited to what I can do!"

Lena was so pissed she hung up the phone on him before he could hang up on her.

"Before you leave, Nasir, Aunt Fran said to call her. She said something about Uncle Stan wants you to come and see him."

"Bet! Where's my nephew?"

"He's with his daddy. I'm using this time to relax. You know responsibility is a motha—"

Mom Flossy's words were hardly mangled when she spoke, "I told you about that shit! Watch your mouth!"

"I'm gone, Grandmom. I hope you had fun." Nasir went inside to give her a kiss.

"I surely enjoyed myself. Next time though, you need to give that girl what she wants. Up there hollering and bickering back and forth. Don't be beggin' so much to put your face in her plate, grandson."

Sheena bent over in laughter.

Nasir was somewhat embarrassed. "Grandmom!" he yelled. "Stop eavesdroppin'."

"Won't no need. You two were that loud. I bet the white family next to Farren's parents' beach house heard y'all too." She turned to Sheena. "You should've heard him, Sheena, trying to make that girl put her mouth of his li'l chicken."

Nasir flew out the door bubblin' from his grandmom's humor. Sheena came laughing behind him. "Don't run now! And, don't forget to call Aunt Fran!"

Nasir put the gearshift in drive. The next stop was to Nakea's to drop off Li'l Marv.

"You want me to take you home before I drop the baby off?"

"Why would you?" Farren's body language was loud.

"Because every time we come from her house, you act all funny and shit. That's why. I'm not for that shit tonight. So, if you plan on acting funny, I'll take you home first."

"I'm ready when you are . . . to drop Li'l Marv off." It was burning her up inside that she had to go through this.

What's Good in the Hood?

The sound systems were battling each other in bass and the females were flexing their little summer tops, showing all the cleavage they could without exposing their nipples. Showing titties was definitely "the thing" this summer; last summer it was showing off your thong. But this summer it was "titty" mania. From 12 years old on up, females were showing their goods. Nasir hadn't seen this much black flesh all week. It was mega white ass at the beach; but this was where it was at—the projects!

The projects had the true, hustlin' women—low income housing and all. They may have lacked in the area of careers, but where they slacked, they definitely made up in getting paid for their creativity—hair, clothes, soul food dinners; keeping the bills paid. By any means, they'd get that shit handled. Nasir admired that in strong independent single-parent women.

"What's up, Nasir?" Shanira winked in his direction. She'd only meet him once and that was through Nakea, but he knew she was riding his nuts. He'd seen the way she examined his rims and his ride, especially how her eye lashes curled the way Lena's did when he came around. She wanted to get stuck by his stick; that's it.

Farren, who was reclined back in the seat, pulled the passenger's seat lever to raise up and answered for Nasir, who was staring directly at the double-slice-pizza pussy print that Shanira had in her tight ass jean shorts, thinking she had to have jumped off a building to fit in those shorts because they were that damn tight. It was no way she put them on by herself. She had help—simple as that.

"Not a damn thing!" Farren fired at Shanira, and then turned to Nasir. "Nasir, do you need me to ring the bell for you?" The disrespect was apparent and she was less than thrilled that he was being so obvious about it. Farren supposed this was the reason he wanted to drop her off. Her once perceived prince charming was turning into a beast—slowly, but surely.

"I got it," he responded and secretly winked back at Shanira, deciding that he would creep back through to see what she was about.

Nasir always made sure Nakea was home before disturbing Li'l Marv if he was asleep. He rang the doorbell twice before Shonda came to the door with a du-rag tied around her head, and cut-off light gray sweat pant shorts, with a white beater T-shirt on.

"Nakea ain't here, but she said to leave Li'l Marv with me." Shonda had the door wide open being nosey.

"I see you carried yo' woman with you again. Tell her she don't have to worry, don't nobody want yo' ass!"

Nasir deliberated whether he should leave his son or not. Shonda was known for leaving her daughter in the house by herself, and he didn't want to make his son victim to that. "What time is she coming back?"

"I don't know. She left out for a few. She'll be right back, damn! Now, like I said, I'll take him."

"That's all right. He can stay with me."

"Nasir, don't be an ass about this. Ain't nothin' gon' happen to that big head boy of yours."

"Yeah, that's what they all say, and next thing you know, you getting a call from the police saying your child has been left unattended."

"Fuck you!" Shonda spat and slammed the door in his face. She knew what he was insinuating.

When Nasir turned to walk back to the car, he was quick with his step. Nakea and Farren were exchanging words and shoves. The music on the block was so loud, he didn't hear the bickering going on.

"Bitch, I don't need you to get my son out the car." Nakea kept reaching for the door handle, but Farren kept using her force to hold it down.

"I said I'd get him out. Now move, tramp!"

"I ain't gon' be to many more tramps, bitch! I'm telling you now. You betta get the fuck outta my way!"

Nasir stepped between them in a sandwich position, much too close to Nakea for Farren. Even though Nakea had moved on and Nasir had treated her ill in the past, it still felt good to her to be up on him this close. She was so close, her face met his.

"Check your woman, Nasir." He could feel the heat rising and smelled Diamonds by Elizabeth Taylor coming out of her pores. His eyes stayed on her, and momentarily, he marveled at the vigor in his baby's mother. That was unexpectedly ended when Farren yanked him away.

"No, you need to school this tramp before I lose it out here."

Nakea's eyes and ears told her what Farren was asking for. That was the last time she was going to call her a tramp. Nakea reached over Nasir and heaved snappily at Farren's head, lodging her body forward, twisting Farren's hair around her hand. Nasir tried to pry free of Nakea's hand, screaming, "Stop it, Nakea, she's pregnant! You can't be fighting a pregnant woman."

Nakea paused in shock and didn't have a chance to dodge the door-blow Farren was coming with . . . *MOCK*! Was the sound echoing from Nakea's eardrum. Li'l Marv had awakened, and began crying loudly. Nasir snatched a bull steaming Farren away, and drove off without dropping his little soldier off to his mother.

"All that talk about losing the baby and you risk the baby's life by fighting?"

"Not right now, Nasir. I seen the way you looked at her. You can have that low-life hoodrat bitch!"

"Yo, why you gotta dis everybody from the projects? Your shit ain't that sweet. If you didn't have your *mommy and daddy* backing you, you might be in the same predicament." He was tired of her always speaking negatively about people that lived in income-assisted housing taking offense to it, because his mother lived in one. Did she think the same about him?

"Am I supposed to feel sorry for them because their mammies ain't shit and they daddies are long gone?" Farren hadn't thought about her rude outburst, causing Nasir to take this to heart.

"I can't believe you, Farren. I thought you were cool peeps. Now, I see otherwise. They say a person can only front for so long before the real person inside of them comes out. I guess I'm seeing the real you."

Farren's face was really distorted from her lack of concern. "You can tell *they* I said FUCK THEM!" Now, drop me the fuck off!"

Nasir didn't know what the hell had gotten into her. If it was the fact that she was pregnant with his child, he wasn't ready for another featured act.

And Then What?

Fed up with Farren and her nasty-ass attitude, Nasir dropped her off at the apartment. Her mood swings were fearless. Just before they went to the beach, they were house shopping, only they weren't buying—they were renting again. They'd seen a nice 3-bedroom house on the outskirts of the city, with brick and stucco surrounding it to strengthen the housing structure. In the front, there was a two-car garage adjacent to a small, filtered water pond to place goldfish in. This was all Farren's idea. Nasir was content with city life, but she insisted that a change in housing was good, now that he had a decent job at Charter Elementary.

Farren had put in her 60-day lease termination notice and agreed to have the landlord show the apartment to perspective tenants for future rental. Nasir didn't agree with that fearing that, their personal belongings would be stolen or tampered with. Plus, he didn't like the fact that someone could find personal information about them from the confines of their apartment. But again, Farren insisted upon helping the landlord find another tenant, because he was good to her during her years of living there.

45

Farren walked up the stairway and she as further neared, she heard voices coming from her apartment.

"Well, thank you very much for allowing me the opportunity to check out this place. Normally, tenants would have a problem with this, but yours must be nice." Lena wooed Dennis Wahl, Farren's landlord, knowing she had no intention on renting out the apartment. When she saw the FOR RENT—OPEN HOUSE sign for the fourth floor apartment, she wasn't letting the opportunity to snoop, go by.

Dennis was eager to keep the rent money going, so he didn't give a damn who he let in. When Lena called to schedule a time with him to see the apartment, after learning Nasir and Farren were not at home, she rushed Dennis over to let her see the place, and he agreed.

"Do you live in the area?" Dennis questioned.

"No, I was riding through and seen the sign." Lena impatiently glanced at her watch. It would only be a short time before Nasir and Farren arrived, if they were headed directly home from Mom Flossy's house. It was merely fifteen miles away.

"Can we make this quick? I have to be to work soon. I wouldn't want to be late . . . gotta pay the bills, you know!" Dennis agreed, opening Farren's apartment door. Lena speedily stepped in.

"Do you mind if I take a quick peek?"

"Sure! Go for it. I'll be in the living room if you have any questions."

Harmony filled Lena's ears as she waltzed to the back bedroom. Regardless of what class she thought Farren had, it changed when she saw the homey looking bed they were sleeping on and those dressers from the late 80's . . . "Damn, Nasir knows better," she mused. In the corner was a wicker laundry basket. Lena opened it up and was greeted by a pair of Farren's thongs. Instead of being apprehensive about it, she was bold, picking up Farren's black thongs and whiffing in a long inhale of *badussy*—ass and pussy scent mixed together— that lingered in them. Lena could also smell Nasir's cum.

The landlord yelled out in concern, "Is everything okay?"

Lena promptly replied, "Yes, I'm good. I'm checking out the closet space," she lied to him. She threw the thongs in her purse. Walking over to the bedroom mirror, with her lipstick in hand, she drew a bleeding heart on it. Nothing else was relevant to her. She got what she came for: an article of clothing of Farren's. Her next stop was to bury them in a cemetery for the death of Nasir and Farren's relationship. That's what a wicked well-experienced spiritual advisor told her to do with them, and she was up on it.

"Well, thank you so much. I appreciate you getting over here so fast. Give me a few days and I'll get back to you."

Dennis shook Lena's hand in disappointment, but hoped she was sincere about calling him back to lease the place. Lena's back was turned facing the door when the knob turned and Farren walked in. Lena almost shit in her pants when the door cracked open. She was cool when she saw it was only Farren.

"Hi, Dennis, I didn't know you were showing the place today." Farren waited for him to answer, but jumped at the chance to greet Lena. "Hey, Ms. Lena, who are you here with?"

"I'm sorry, Farren. I know I usually give you a 24-hour notice, but this was like a spur of the moment showing," Dennis apologized. "This nice woman was checking the place out to possibly rent it."

Farren was puzzled gazing at Lena. "Well, unless she's selling her house, I don't know why she would rent this out?"

Lena's little mini-skirt with her strapless top was killing it for a woman her age. She was an aged dime piece. Farren watched her sway from side to side, but her parameters were well off.

"No honey, this is way too small for me. Quinton is searching for a place. I figured the rent is cheap and the size is just right for him." Lena knew how crazy

Farren had been about her son, and this story was very believable.

"Wouldn't it be a bit strange with him moving into my old apartment?"

Lena scanned Farren's body and noticed how hammy she'd become—the same way she looked when she was pregnant by Quinton. "Why would it be strange, darling?"

The landlord was totally clueless.

"You and Quinton broke this apartment in, remember? I'm sure he'd loved to relive the memories. By the way, you are looking a bit thick-ish. You're not attempting to have a baby again, *are you*?"

Farren's face changed colors quickly. She couldn't believe Ms. Lena was speaking so frankly. "Ms. Lena, I'm not attempting, I *am* having a baby. Isn't that wonderful?"

Lena clutched her pocketbook and thought, *Not for long.* But what escaped out of her mouth was, "If you say so." She turned to Dennis and said, "I must get going. I have someplace to be. Like I said, I'll be in touch . . . Dennis, right?"

"Yes." He nodded.

"I thought that's what I heard princess call you." She knew how much Farren was against being called by the nickname Quinton had given her for her "your highness" ways.

Lena and Dennis walked out leaving Farren to herself. She was so overwhelmed; she took a shower then went into the bedroom with an unmoving face. She stared at the bleeding heart on the mirror.

What the hell! What is this about? Farren thought, leaving the artwork untouched. She made it home before Nasir, so he couldn't have done it. Maybe it was someone Dennis showed the house to. This had to be the reason Nasir was dead set against letting people coming into the place while they were still living there—this type of shit. Tomorrow she would make a call to Dennis to find out who he had in the apartment.

After her discovery, she crashed in the living room waiting for Nasir to come home to continue their argument. Now, she had another issue to fuss about.

Can You Hear Me Now?

"Do you want to get dat bitch today or tomorrow?" Shonda was ready to get at Farren after sitting in the emergency room for over four hours with Nakea for a perforated eardrum. Farren had temporarily knocked the sound out of Nakea's left ear. Shonda had dropped her daughter off with her mother, Daisy, for the time being.

Nakea couldn't differentiate her feelings about her ear and the news of Farren expecting a baby.

"That bitch is pregnant, Shonda. We can go to jail if we hit her."

"Fuck dat! Was she worried about that when she busted your ear out?"

Nakea was driven by her desire to make Farren pay at this very moment. "You're right, the bitch deserves everything that's coming to her! Let's cancel that ho!" Her left ear was still ringing from the hella hit Farren placed on her.

☙☙☙☙☙

Nasir had stopped by Loretta's for her to keep Li'l Marv for a few. He knew when he called Nakea's house and Sean answered, he wouldn't stand a chance of

51

speaking with her. Sean blocked any and all conversation he could between them.

"Listen, playboy, Nakea ain't here and I ain't watchin' some otha nigga's baby. That ain't my job, son."

"Man, I don't need you to watch my seed! I called to ask for his mother, if she ain't home, I'll check for her later, partna!"

"Listen here, ain't gon' be too much phone callin' in *my* crib. We can establish that shit right now. Y'all need to decide a neutral place for her to pick up that baby . . . 'cause, Money . . . you ain't welcomed here!" Sean never recognized Li'l Marv by his name, always addressing him as "that baby" because he was that petty when it came to Nasir, and he picked up on it.

"My mothafuckin' son's name is Marvin—Li'l Marv at that, nigga! It's okay to say my government name. That's my little soldier. You fuck your girl right like I did, and maybe, you can get a seed outta her too, nigga!" he bragged in an ego statement to Sean.

"Suck my dick, faggot!" Sean stated harshly while hanging up. Nakea was getting her ass beat again when she came home just for that.

Meanwhile, Nasir had other stops to make and he didn't want to take Li'l Marv. That's why he went to his mom's house.

"Mom, how you livin'?" Since he had moved out he barely had conversation with Loretta, holding her actions true to heart from the family court hearing. "Have you talked to your non-biological daughter today? I've been trying to drop Li'l Marv off."

Loretta reached for Li'l Marv, and with him in her bosom, this was her chance to check Nasir.

"Court order states 6 p.m. Its 10 p.m. and he's still not in his mother's custody."

"Damn! You policing me?" He frowned. "For your information, I attempted to drop him off, twice!"

"Yes, I know, but Farren perforated Nakea's eardrum when she hit her, and Nakea is at the hospital. You better know it—she's pressing charges against her."

"What?"

"Yes, negro, she is. And I don't give a flying shit about Farren *supposedly* being pregnant. She had no business putting her hands on that girl. She deserves to be arrested!"

"Mom, you don't what you're talking about. You always get a half-ass story and side with that girl."

"Yes, the hell I do. Nakea called me from the hospital and told me everything. She'll be here when she leaves the hospital to pick up my grandson."

"Let me ask you something, Mom, why do you always act like what Nakea says is written in the sky? You're always siding with that girl."

"I'm not always siding with her, but right is right and wrong is wrong!"

"I agree with you one hundred percent. So, what's your problem admitting that you are dead-ass wrong when it comes to dealing with your own blood?"

Loretta went into reactionary mode. "I didn't receive the memo on that!"

"You never do when it comes to us. One day you'll receive a cruel awakening."

Nasir exited her house, ready to trick with Lena. He had to release his built-up tension.

AT THE COURT'S MERCY

Ah, how good it feels!

The hand of an old friend.

Henry Wadsworth Longfellow

It's a Family Affair

Strange as it may seem, Nasir felt closer in spirit with his father when he was with Lena. When they were together, she would play the oldies, but goodies radio station, or pull out her vinyl records; the 45's and 33's, not needing to invest in CD's because she had her classic form of music, that had the original static melody. She reminisced about Big Marv, shared photos, and often told Nasir stories he'd never heard. From what his mother told him, his father only had a life with her. But boy was Loretta wrong, or his mom intentionally hid that from him—he wasn't sure. Big Marv took care of home nonetheless, but there were others who benefited too.

"Your father never would've let your mother carry on like she does now." Nasir watched Lena as she bent over in her white thong and matching robe, exposing her breasts that had two little white star pasties attached on each nipple, to get her slippers. He was spread out across the bed ass naked, ready to hit some skins, but Lena was running her mouth a bit too much, ruining his dirty, lustful thoughts.

"Be quiet and stay right there in that position."

AT THE COURT'S MERCY

She turned to slightly face him; still with her ass in the air.

"You should probably hold onto the dresser, because when this wood gets up in you, you'll need to hold onto something for life."

Lena loved when he talked like a thugged out nigga with a strong back. She wanted him to beat it up— wasn't no soft passionate love making going on between them. It was strictly a fuck session—ass slapping, sweaty palms, heads banging, loud grunting noises and some serious toes curling up. They had "live wire" sessions.

Nasir stroked his johnson until it reached the max of stiffness. He stood in back of Lena, and with the pull of his index finger, he slid her thong over, and thrusted himself against the moistness between her legs. For the first time, he didn't use a condom to protect himself. He wanted to feel every inch of her nasty, old ass; thinking with his wrong head.

When their bodies combined it became quite violent. Nasir plunged deeper and deeper inside her sugar walls. As Nasir predicted, Lena's head began to bang against her dresser. Nasir was watching the work he was putting in though a full view mirror that connected to the dresser. His intensity grew as he felt like he was "the man," beating the hell out of a woman his mother's age. This old head's pussy made him fill with pride.

Lena felt that he would cum soon and didn't want to miss this opportunity of him ejaculating in her. So, she lifted up, causing Nasir's eyebrows to raise in question. With a quickness, she pushed him to the edge of the bed and hopped on top and began to ride him until he went limp. This time, she was in control, and knew when he came, it would explode all in her. After they were finished, he went about his way.

For every minute you remain angry, you give up sixty seconds of peace of mind.

Ralph Waldo Emerson

Blast from the Past

Loretta was in the grocery store, late night, when she did her shopping. After Nakea was released from the hospital, she came to pick up Li'l Marv a half an hour after Nasir had dropped him off, so Loretta was able to grab items off the grocery list she made.

Marking items off, Loretta wasn't bothering anyone; unemotionally, she was idly in her own mind, thinking about her relationship with her children. Sheena hadn't talked to her—for all that she didn't do for her. And when it came to Nasir, it was that damn Farren that came and interrupted their bond. If she'd never been in Nasir's life, Nakea and him would still be together. She knew that in her heart. That's why she kept telling Nakea to grin and bear it; Nasir would come home. She'd hoped when she got on the witness stand that Li'l Marv would be awarded to his mother's custody. That way, Nakea would have the upper hand. When it backfired, she knew she had to rethink how she would pull Farren and Nasir apart.

So caught up in her thinking, Loretta's shopping cart hit the heels of another shopper. As she mouthed, "I'm sorry," to the woman she'd backed up on, her apology turned sour.

AT THE COURT'S MERCY

"Well, well, well, if it isn't Miss Ho-stroll." Lena stepped to the side of the cart, giving Loretta a full body view of her. It wasn't a coincidence that she was there. She had been following Loretta's patterns for two weeks now. This was exactly what she planned to do; accidentally bump into her. Just by chance, Loretta fell right into her trap.

Loretta hadn't seen Lena since she'd been home from prison and was instantly jealous of the sleeveless red camisole that exposed Lena's red padded pushup bra, giving her aged breasts a lift. She had gracefully blossomed into a woman in her forties.

"Who the fuck is you calling ho-stroll, whore?" Loretta's immediate fury was imminent to this troublemaker.

"Cut that tough-girl act out, Loretta. That's been played out. Ain't no bullies no more—scared kids are killing them off."

Loretta shifted the cart to move ahead, but Lena moved with her, gripping the front of it.

"How about we play a little game?"

"Bitch, you better move before I ram this cart inside your stomach!" Loretta was mentally shattered, trying to piece herself back together.

Lena was certainly off the mark interfering with Loretta's personal time. "Oh, come on, Loretta . . . for the sake of love, play the damn game. You may discover some startling news." She wanted to teach Loretta a lesson, and the deep penetrating gaze she had on her face wasn't going anywhere, until she heard her out. However, Loretta wouldn't cooperate. "Are you sure you don't wanna play?"

Loretta tried to move the cart again.

"Okay, well let me help you out. Maybe this little rhyme will get your attention. Roses are red, violets are blue. I fucked Marv. Sr., and your baby boy too!"

Lena's infectious laughter ricocheted through the aisle of the supermarket, leaving Loretta stinging in hatred.

At the oddest moment Loretta waned, shoving the cart from in front of her, chasing behind Lena who quickly trotted off.

"I'ma kill you, bitch!!!" Loretta screamed as patrons watched her act like a wild woman.

Not for nothing, though. This was what Loretta needed to get Farren out of her son's life. She knew damn well Farren didn't know about this.

When we started, it was based on lies.
It's changing now.

Don King

It's Not About Me

After the weekend was over and after all of the chaos between Nakea and Farren, Nasir chose to meet Nakea at his mom's to gather his son. The battle between the two women was hardly over. Farren had yet to turn herself in, thinking that Nakea's claim to have signed a warrant on her was bogus. She went to work, still acting like a bitch toward Nasir.

For the most part, Nasir kept Li'l Marv with him. But the days he had to oversee the Gentlemen's program, the summer program he began for Charter Elementary, he took him to Lois Kiddie 1, 2, 3; one of the best home daycare's in the city. Nasir didn't trust anybody but the affectionate, loving woman, Mrs. Lois Stovall, who cared for his son, other than his mother and Farren.

Today though, he had plenty of time to spend with his son since his schedule was open. It was mutually agreed between Nakea and Nasir, since Farren was the cause of her losing weekend time with the baby that she would keep him until Monday morning. From her visit to the emergency room, Nakea was given five days off of work. However, it was her responsibility, even after taking painkillers, to get her ass up bright and early to meet Nasir. It had to be every bit of 9 a.m. when Nasir arrived to his mother's. Waiting patiently, he flicked the channel button, settling for ESPN previews. He laughed at how ridiculous Terrell Owens was acting, having tantrums against the Eagles' coach, Andy Reed, for not giving him more money on his contract.

"Come on, Terrell, that's a bitch move," he said aloud.

Ever since Nasir moved in with Farren, Loretta wanted her house key back. There wasn't a need for him to come in and out of her house freely, when he stopped paying the bills. With a pink robe on, Loretta tied her belt together around her waist, and went to boil some hot water for her morning tea.

"What are you doing here so early on a Monday morning?"

"Good morning, Mom," Nasir greeted her, even though she wasn't fond of greeting him in return.

"Didn't I tell you months ago to give me my key back? I'ma have the locks changed. That will fix that."

"Do you wake up every morning with a plan to tear your kids down?"

"No, just some days." She went along with him.

"I can't tell. You never have one good thing to say to us. It would be nice for once if you said: Hi . . . hello

. . . good morning. How's the job coming along? Instead of: what you doing here?"

"Nakea must be bringing the baby over here." She sat her gold ceramic mug down on the counter to place her tea bag in it. "That's the only time you come over here. When you need to use my house for safe grounds," she expressionlessly stated.

Loretta was accurate. Their mother and son relationship had dwindled to nothing more than coming together for a meeting spot.

"You made it that way. Anyway, Nakea is on her way, so please don't start it up."

"This is my got damn house. I'll start whatever the hell I want to up in here," she replied, sipping her tea slowly to avoid burning her lips from its hotness. "I got a serious bone to pick with you anyhow. What the fuck is this I hear that you are fucking old ass Lena?"

Nasir's body stiffened, and for a few seconds he didn't know what to say. *How did his mother find out?* he thought. Not even a handful of people knew about their secret affair.

"I don't even know no woman named Lena."

"Stop fucking lying to me. You know that shriveled up whore. If your father were alive, he would beat the shit outta of you for messing with that. You better hope you don't catch worms from her corroded insides."

"Damn, whoever she is, you sure don't like her."

"You have one more time to act like you don't know that woman, and I'ma throw this boiling pan of hot water on your ass. Try me, mothafucka!"

Nasir could see that his mother was not playing. Evidently, this bothered her deeper than he thought it would.

"Whoa now!" He stood up to face her. "Okay, I do know her, but that's it."

"Nigga, see!" Loretta started screaming, picking up the pan bubbling with hot water.

"Mom! Mom! All right . . . All right. I did fuck her!"

"You dirty dick bastard!" Loretta began to cry. "Do you know what the woman has taken me through? She's the same bitch that called you a *trick baby,* and now you're fucking her?"

"How was I to know about what happened in the past? You don't ever tell me shit about my father but that he was a good man."

"Nasir, your father cheated on me with her. She tried everything in her power to steal your father away from me! She may even have a . . ." Loretta ran off to her room, leaving Nasir baffled by their conversation.

What else did she have to say? he wondered.

Nasir left the door unlocked for Nakea. Perhaps them meeting like this strengthened their failing courtship. They were on meager speaking terms. Both of them knew the importance of following the court order and neither wanted to breach it, so they both played their roles. It may not have been sincere from either one of them, but even with fronting, it seemed righteous.

In front of Loretta's house, Li'l Marv was making playful noises, laughing at his mother for putting her face on his stomach like she was trying to blow bubbles on it. Her son was what helped her heart to keep beating. He made her life worth living. Her mother, Daisy, had totally cut down the branches from her tree, leaving Shonda and Nakea out there. On occasion, she would let her grandkids come over, but it was only for a few hours—never overnight. Nakea and Shonda didn't even try to force them on her.

Nakea pushed the door opened with her feet, carrying a baby bag, car seat, and the baby in her arms. "Hey, Nasir, where's your mom?"

"Back in her room." He searched her from top to bottom.

"See something you like?"

Figures, she thought. *When I didn't have a man, and was sweatin' him, he wouldn't give me the time of day. Now that I got my own place, my own car, and a good job, nigga all up on me. Shit, he supposed to love me now! Back then, he didn't want me. Now that I'm hot, he's all on me.* She smiled within. *Mike Jones was hella right when he made that song.*

"Not, hardly. I see you on the come up though!"

"Whateva! Just 'cause you got a little job at that school, it don't make you the man. And while we're having civil conversation, you know you dead wrong for filing for child support, when you know I take care of my son!"

"Women do it all day long. Why shouldn't I? I have custody of him. The least you can do is pay some support. If you can't pay, tell ya nigga to pay it. Oops, I'm sorry, dat nigga's broke!"

"Sound like somebody is jealous if you ask me," Loretta said, going to pick up Li'l Marv from the blue-and-yellow fabric car seat; not showing Nakea that she was upset with Nasir.

"And do!" Nakea agreed. "I'm sorry, but I gotta man, boo-boo." She laughed in his face.

"I don't want your stank-ass anyway." He gripped his bulge between his legs. "You try to be nice and that gets taken as you wantin' to get back—nah, never that. 'I don't take 'em out to eat. I don't take 'em trick or treat. I ain't here to fix their weave. I'on do none of that'," he rhymed Slim Thugs lyrics.

Nakea looked to Loretta. "See, that's the young boy in him. Told you . . . him getting that job didn't make him mature."

"Gimme my son and let me get outta here 'fore I say somethin' to both of y'all. Oh yeah, you need to drop those charges against Farren too. I went up City Hall too and they confirmed that you did press charges."

"What? You thought it was a joke? Not on my life! I had to get her first, before she went down there on me. This way, if future occurrences happen, Nakea is covered. I'll holla! Miss Loretta, I'll call you later. I'm trying to enjoy my week off. Thanks to Farren."

"She is not your friend. One day you'll learn that. My mom don't care about nobody but herself."

"That's what you say. She looks out for me. Don't you, Miss Loretta?"

"Of course, baby." Loretta confirmed, screw-facing Nasir. "Be sure to call me too, I have something to *tell* you!"

"I should have known . . . meager minds think alike," Nasir uttered the honest truth.

There's nothing wrong with getting knocked down, as long as you get right back up.

Muhammed Ali

Can I get my grown man on?

"Aunt Fran, what you need baby? Sheena told me you called, paroling about me?"

"Young boy, please. I'm not one of your little fans. I called you because your Uncle Stan wants to see you, and to let you know that I added you to his visitor's list.

"A'ight. I'll call and make a visit."

"No need; did that too. It's this Saturday at 10 a.m. Be there at 9:45 a.m. or those bastards won't let you in. Make sure you have your ID. You do have one, don't you?"

"Why wouldn't I, Aunt Fran? Only people doing wrong don't carry identification. I'm on the right track. I know you peeped me in my suit at the school when you rode past that day. I seen you and your little friend."

"Your father used to wear suits just like that, but he slicked his out with hats. Y'all young boys don't know anything about that. Swear y'all got the game sewed up, when you're broke, busted and disgusted. Feel me?" she teased him with some slang. "And don't be worrying about who's in my car! Keep ya mouth shut too!"

"I feel ya, ma," Nasir teased her back.

"Can I preach?"

"Do you, baby! Do you!" was Nasir's reply.

"Then let me . . . yeah, and what about the problems y'all create with these young girls? Feed 'em a bunch of lies, then expect your shit to be sweet when you done using them. Then you wonder why you have all this drama—I tell you! Somebody needs to teach y'all young boys something, and fast. At the rate black men are going, it ain't gon' be too many good ones left."

"Aunt Fran, come on back, baby. I'm sure Uncle Stan will understand if you make that *good man* you had in your car your new partner."

"Hush, boy, just make sure you get to the prison early for the visit, and keep your mouth shut!"

"I will."

"You do that," she chuckled. "Where you off to now?"

"I need to stop by the school and check up on a few students that are in the Gentlemen's summer program."

"That's good. I'm proud of you, Nasir. I know it was hard making the switch from your previous job."

"Yeah," he mumbled to her. "It sure was. I'll catch you later, Aunt Fran."

Now he was rushing her off the phone. Although he was pleased to hear the words, 'I'm proud of you,' he knew she would be hurt if she found out that he was still involved in the game. Really, quite a few good people who were behind him would be disappointed: Professor Hurdle and Principal Hurdle, her husband. That gave him a second chance in life to make good. What would happen if he blew it?

Working at the school was his first real job with good pay and benefits. His son didn't want for anything, and Nakea didn't have to resort to the State to get help. He'd only filed for child support to spite her—take her through some drama like she had taken him. He remembered the day she called him, pissed off when she received the petition for child support.

"How could dis nigga stoop so low?" Nakea threw the letter across the room. Shonda snatched it up when it hit the floor, simply replying, "That boy gon' pay for this."

"He's only doing this outta animosity. He knows damn well I don't make that much from Amazon's warehouse."

"I guess he figured Sean's giving you money to help maintain you."

"I don't give a fuck! That doesn't have anything to do with him asking for support."

"I told you . . . you gotta play dirty like these niggas. If it was me, I'd been set his ass up! My child would be back with me. Humph! And, you got a place too? I don't see why he ain't back here yet. Wait 'til my Section 8 fall through. I'm transferring my shit to Atlanta."

"Bullshit, you are! You would leave me like that?"

"Without thinking twice, bitch!"

"Who you know in Atlanta?"

"My girl, Nicalett, moved down there, and her sister Tiny hooked me up with her number. You remember them, don't you?"

"Yeah, sorta. Is their mom named Ms. Linda?"

"Yeah. Nicalett said it's easy to find housing. All you need is a voucher and you could get a phat ass crib. Not no shit like this."

They were sitting in the living room with the shades lifted all the way up, looking at drug sales being made right in front of Nakea's house. Across the street, a crackhead woman named Bones lived with her son, Tyaire, and a house full of roomers that were drug addicts. Tyaire was out all hours of the night roaming the streets when the house was in session, and that was damn near all the time.

"I don't wanna raise my daughter in the projects. Look at this shit!" she pointed to Bones and a dealer selling her crack. "Bones' son is living fucked up. I don't want my daughter to become victim to this. I know I smoke a little weed, but that's about it. Fuck living like this! The projects ain't a place to raise your kids. I mean, if that's all I got, then it'll work; but if I can get a townhouse and get out the PJ's (projects), you wouldn't be able to tell me jack!"

Nakea's eyes started darting back and forth from the outside, to her sister, feeling offended. "I understand all what you saying, but at least I got a place! Housing ain't my issue; it's Nasir with this child support shit. That's what the fuck we was talkin' 'bout. I can't help Bones with her situation, when mine is fucked up. But um, back to Nasir, he went too far. Lemme call this nigga!"

When Nakea called him, she cussed him out until he hung up on her. She was steaming for a minute.

৶৶৶৶৶

Nasir took each concrete step with stride as his feet touched them; knocking on the door of Lois Kiddie 1, 2, 3. Mrs. Lois came to the door. She smiled lovingly and took Li'l Marv inside.

"Thanks, Mrs. Lois. I'll be by to get him around 5 p.m."

"I'll see you then," she said, closing the door while the other kids tried to sneak a peak at the person on the other side of the door.

76

AT THE COURT'S MERCY

Working at the school, Nasir surfaced as a young African-American male, proud to be employed in a job he enjoyed. He found his passion working with inner city youth, as he was. Many of them reminded him of himself as a lad. Most of the boys were growing up without fathers or with chemical dependant mothers, and some, without either.

This is what prompted him to run the Gentlemen's program. He may have been swimming in dangerous water; however, this was a way for him to give back. Nasir approached Principle Hurdle with the idea and he let him run with it. Sending out letters to each male student's home, Nasir feared the program wouldn't be received. But before the week was out, over seventy boys enrolled with parental consent. This huge turnout wasn't expected, and Nasir had to call on others to help him run it.

On one end of the spectrum he was a hood— dealing in the drug game, chasing the all mighty dollar and sexual thrills; and on the other end, he was teaching young males about proper hygiene, self-respect, hygiene, and knowledge of self. Sometimes, he'd even take them on special outings if their behavior warranted; changing tempos like night and day. Both worlds he was addicted to. He loved the satisfying feeling.

"Are all the Gentlemen lined up in the gym?" Nasir directed his question to one of his strongest linemen.

"Yes, Mr. B," a nappy, sandy brown hair little boy named Tyaire responded.

All of the boys knew Nasir as Mr. B. They never called him by his full last name: Bundy.

"Good going, Tyaire. Let's get the game started then." With the help Instructor Brad, an asset to the program, they introduced to the group the game of chess. The game lasted a half hour; from highly intense games, to losers wanting to run the game back to beat their opponent.

"The strategy of the game is to learn how to out think your opponent to get to their king. If you know what their next move is going to be, chances are, you've out-smarted them. Remember, you want to be king of their throne as well as yours," Instructor Brad explained to them. Principle Hurdle passed by the gym and watched Nasir, Instructor Brad and the group members, play with intense faces. It did his heart good to see knuckleheads content and willing to participate in a game of chess. This was the second time in years he'd seen a male figure touch the young male's hearts the way Nasir did, the first time he did. He believed Nasir was well on his way to becoming an affluent staff member in the educational system, if he buckled down and went to college to obtain a degree. Without one, he wouldn't be fully equipped to teach or be able to make the money he deserved, if he didn't remain focused.

"All right, players, its wrap up time until next session."

Nasir left from the school with one passenger in tow: Tyaire. No one showed to take him home, so he volunteered to give him a ride. Although he had no idea Tyaire lived in the same development as Nakea. He'd never seen him over there.

"Mr. B, can I ask you a personal question?" Tyaire challenged his eyes to meet Nasir's. "Was that you I seen on Friday in my projects?" Nasir didn't want to lie to him, but knew when he pulled directly across the street from Nakea's to Tyaire's house, that it might have been possible that Tyaire saw him.

"Maybe, Tye. I'm not sure."

"Do you live in the projects Mr. B? Or were you just riding through? Everybody be coming through our set in hot rides!" The fascination of a hustler was all in Tyaire's eyes.

"Nah, I was visiting with someone."

"Oh . . . was that someone the woman that got knocked the fuck out?"

"Whoa, baby, you talkin' crazy now." The car was in park. "Are your parent's home?" Tyaire was procrastinating getting out of the car.

"If I tell you this, Mr. B, you ain't gon' rank on me, are you?"

"Of course not." Nasir felt saddened for Tyaire, hoping that his living conditions weren't that bad.

"My mom's a crackhead and my dad's in jail for seven years. All the kids tease me about them. I hate coming home. We never have anything to eat, and my mom is always crying broke. If God were to grant me one wish, it would be for my mom to leave drugs alone. She was a good mom before she started getting high."

Nasir sympathized with him. "Are you hungry now?"

"Yes."

"Well, I can't leave you with hunger pains. Let's hit the steak shop and get you a large cheese steak. How's that sound?"

Tyaire rubbed his belly. "That sounds delicious. I haven't had a cheese steak since the last time they served it for lunch, when school was in."

They pulled away, never noticing Sean peep their every move. He sat in Nakea's window wondering why Nasir was parked in his car, spying on them. What was he up to? He speculated that Nasir was trying to get back with his woman. With crazed vengeance, Sean began to plot.

I can only see it going one way, that's my way. How it's actually going to go, I can't really say.
Nick Wilshire

No More Drama? . . .

I don't think so!

"I told you not to fuck wit' me, didn't I? You had to take me there!" Nakea wilded out on Farren. Punching and kicking the shit out of her with the help of Shonda, who was spitting all in her face.

"Pull her up! Let me get the bitch good—one good time," Shonda said with a dangling white string of spit hanging from her mouth.

Poor Farren had just gotten off of work, dressed to the nines in a tailored black Travis Ayers double-breasted suit, with one-and-a-half inch new black Nine West mules on. If Nasir had a clue what was happening, he would be in a panic. Farren was eight weeks pregnant. Both of them knew the risks, and had to take every precautionary method to keep the fetus safe until Farren's cervix could get sewn together. She'd miscarried before on two occasions with Quinton's babies, and risked losing her love child with Nasir. She fought back, but Nakea and Shonda's teamwork had knocked her almost literally, the fuck

out. She couldn't fight them back like she wanted to—
if she wanted to—she was an expectant mother.

Nakea yanked Farren by the head, snapping her
neck back. Farren could see Shonda as she reared
back her right leg. Her eyes closed to alleviate
watching the horror of her body being victimized.
Shonda made sure she gave herself dancing room after
she put the finishing touches on the can of whip-ass
that she and Nakea had put on her.

Whomp! Whomp! Whomp! Was the sound heard
when the air brushed past Farren. Aiming merciless to
knock the life out of Farren, Shonda's size ten
Timberland boots, flickered back twice before kicking
Farren: once in her side and once in her pelvic area,
crouching Farren to the ground.

"Now, who gets the last laugh, bitch! Huh?"
Shonda tormented her helpless prey. "I told you to stay
the fuck outta this, but you had to keep runnin' your
uppity mouth!"

Sonya and Chauncey happened to be driving pass
the divided overpass which Greyhound was near, when
they noticed Farren getting a number put on her.

"Stop the car! Stop the car! I wanna see this."
Sonya was glad that she was a witness to this fight.
She wanted a taste of Farren for stealing her young
boy. This beat down was one she didn't want to miss.

"Yo, ain't that Nasir's girl?" Chauncey squinted, pulling his shoulders close to the steering wheel of his Cadillac Seville sedan.

"Yeah, that's the bitch, and that's his baby momma and her sister, Shonda, beatin' her ass too." She laughed.

"Dem bitches wrong for jumpin' her like that. Coward bitches, bet they wouldn't fight her one on one."

Sonya chin-checked Chauncey with her eyes. "What, you got it bad for her too? Why you talkin' in her defense? That bitch got somethin' on you?" He knew of Sonya's constant insecurities of Farren from the meaningless gossip that she always spread about her.

Chauncey pulled the car over; not to watch, but to come to Farren's aid. Throwing the car in park, he jumped out of the car, running in between two oncoming cars to get to her. By this time, Farren's supervisor had come to help, prohibiting others from being spectators to this event.

If the supervisor had worked overtime as he normally did, he would have never saved Farren from her ill-fated incident. When he saw what was transpiring, he stopped the nonsense and immediately gathered Farren up to take her to the nearest hospital.

"Get your hands off of her before I call the police!" David, Farren's supervisor screamed in warning, trying to force them to leave.

"Fuck you, tighty whitey," Shonda yelled, pulling Nakea up the block. "She got what she deserved, let's go!"

Sonya hollered to Chauncey, "Let's get the fuck out of here before the po-po come. I ain't try'na go in for questioning. I ain't see shit!"

Chauncey reached the car taking another look at Farren, whose face was grimaced—moaning and still folded over in pain. Sonya's ultimate satisfaction was seeing Farren in such a way. Putting the car in gear, Chauncey released his hazard lights and turned the volume to his CD player on high.

"You think she gon' be all right?" he asked with his poker face, trying to feel Sonya out.

"Fuck that, bitch! Who cares if she's not, you? 'Cause I don't!"

❧❧❧❧❧

Farren was seen immediately in the OB/GYN unit at the emergency room. The moment she demonstrated her loyalty and devotion to Nasir, her life became overwhelmed with unnecessary bullshit from the constant games that Nakea kept playing. But she never feared that her life would be in danger when dealing with her. This time, Nakea and Shonda probably made the worst mistake of them all.

David personally accompanied Farren. And upon reaching the hospital, he called her parents to be by her side, before he left. He was much too familiar with Nakea from her false threats and complaints to the corporate office about Farren. She'd caused Farren from receiving a promotion that was deserving of her, and even was a key element in the company's decision to demote her for her involvement in an argument with Nakea, in front of the Greyhound offices.

It was a Thursday evening and Farren had a wonderful successful day. She'd secured ten buses, filling every seat. When an employee did that, they'd receive one comp day off for each bus they filled. Farren had shocked herself by being awarded ten comp days. As soon as she walked outside for a break, she was faced with a bad situated that aired constant conflict. Instead of going back inside to handle it appropriately, she challenged Nakea, ready to handle it her way.

"What do you want?" Farren asked in noticeable hostility.

"Bitch, who da fuck you think you are?" Nakea approached her with fierceness piercing through her eyes.

AT THE COURT'S MERCY

"I'm, Farren, trick. Don't get it confused." They stood face to face. "Why do you keep stalking me? I'm not the one who fucked you and left you—it was Nasir!"

Nakea bit her tongue. "I bet you feel good poppin' that shit, but how do you think your boss is going to handle it when I tell him you turned a paying customer away? I didn't come here to bother you. I came to purchase bus tickets, bitch!"

If that was the case, Nakea had a legitimate complaint this time. Instead of doing as Nasir informed her to, and play on Nakea's insecurities, she continued to let Nakea do that to her. Farren made a critical mistake. Nakea wasn't as dumb as Farren thought. She had sense enough to harass Farren, stop her from getting a promotion and eventually, causing her a demotion, due to the ongoing confrontations they had while Farren was on the job. She had unquestionably gotten under her skin.

෴෴෴෴෴

As soon as Nasir received a call from the hospital, he immediately placed a call to Mrs. Lois.

"Mrs. Lois, Farren is in the hospital. If I pay you an additional twenty dollars, can you can keep Li'l Marv until I find out what's up with her?"

"Sure, baby. Take your time. You know he's in good hands," she said as she watched Li'l Marv sleeping away in the Blue's Clues playpen.

In twenty minutes, Nasir reached the corridor of the hospital that Farren was in. At the general information desk, he was pointed in the direction of the emergency room where Farren was in Room 13. Approaching, Nasir could hear very loud, excruciating screams of pain. That voice was none other than Farren's. He slightly knocked on the closed door and made his way in. A young black male resident doctor named Wayne was reading off the chart, sharing the grave results. He stopped talking when Nasir barged in. "I'm Nasir, Farren's partner."

Farren was peering toward the dark painted walls with her knees pulled tightly to her chest. Her hair was muddled and she had red bruises on her face, neck and arms. There was another slight knock at the door. Again, Doctor Wayne turned to face the door. It was Farren's mother, Leslie, and her father, Raymond. With no delay, Leslie ran over to console her daughter, fingering her hair back and wiping her tears. Farren was in hysterics. Her sight was temporary blinded; her body numb and she had lost the ability to articulate what was real versus what wasn't. Nasir didn't know what to say or do.

"Please tell us what happened to our daughter." Leslie considered it necessary to be informed.

Doctor Wayne thoughtfully prepared and chose his words carefully.

"I'm sorry to inform you, Farren . . ." he sighed and corrected himself, "Miss Giles lost the baby."

Nasir's knees buckled and Raymond heaved his body up.

"Pregnant?" Both she and her husband were unaware of this. Farren hadn't told them yet.

"She wasn't gonna tell you until she had the procedure to help keep the baby up in there; fearing if she told you too early, she may have a miscarriage," Nasir put it in plain words for them of his understanding of what Farren had to go through to prevent losing the baby.

When Doctor Wayne finished explaining to them the dangers of Farren's future pregnancies, Leslie cried out, "My baby may never have kids?"

Farren screamed vociferously, changing everyone's spirit to heartache. This was the third time that she'd lost a baby, but that wasn't even the worst of it. One of her ovaries was bruised and there was a strong possibility that physically, she may never carry a baby full-term.

David was worried about her outcome. If only he'd saved her sooner. His thoughts reflected on seeing the happiness written all over Farren's face, when she told her co-workers that she had a surprise to tell them; but it had to wait a few weeks. Most of them knew how bad she wanted a baby. That was fifty percent of her conversation when she did chit-chat with them. However, after seeing Farren getting plummeted, David knew if she were pregnant, the baby wouldn't survive a beating as intense as that.

"Anybody know what caused this?" The news hadn't traveled through the mill thus far. Nasir was hurting with his woman. He'd never seen her in this state before. But her mother and father had.

Both miscarriages, prior to this one, were traumatic for Farren. Each time weighed heavier in distress. She was told after her first miscarriage, everything would be okay the next time. Farren clung tight to those words and tried not to get locked into the sadness and frustration that the loss made her feel. The annihilation of feeling failure became harder to cope with when she was trying to have a positive outlook toward future pregnancies. It was increasingly difficult to come to grips with—an emotional and lonely experience. The thought of the unknown—what could have been—was tagged onto her hardship.

When other women were around her with babies, she admired seeing mother and child at first, but that admiration quickly turned to envy, not showing the same enthusiasm she once had.

After the first loss, it was even difficult for her to go into stores that sold baby products, but the torment eased when she found out she was pregnant for a second time.

Despite what Farren felt about Quinton, he was there for her, both physically and mentally. He was a dog, but he wasn't an insensitive man. He catered to her every need during both upsetting ordeals. Besides, he was a father and couldn't make out losing his daughter, so he sympathized with his Farren.

When they found out she was expecting the second time, Quinton called himself romancing her; taking her out to the Riverfront attractions, watching the fireworks lakeside during the Fourth of July celebrations. They sat on the grass on a thick blanket, and cuddled while he rubbed her stomach, delightfully embracing each other in love.

Subsequently, four weeks later, Farren felt cramping. A week after that, she started passing blood clots and had a fever of 101.4 degrees. The following night, she miscarried in Quinton's bathroom and had to be rushed to the hospital for a D&C—dilation and curettage—to remove any fetal or placental tissue that was still inside.

The aftermath of the second miscarriage doubled in sorrow for the bereaving couple. Farren had sleepless, depressing nights. Her persistent fears, nervousness, panic and unusual thoughts, eventually led her to a nervous breakdown. That's when the collapse of her and Quinton's relationship began. Instead of bonding with him, Farren lashed out at him, blaming him when he wasn't to blame. At first, he brushed it off, but after months of depression and hateful comments from Farren about his daughter's mother, he started sleeping around on her. The down spiral began. Farren found out and kicked him to the curb; never really putting an end to their relationship.

Leslie decided it was best that her daughter sought out counseling. They arranged the first meeting and were there as stable support. It took six months of delicate counseling before Farren minimized the doubts of her femininity, guilt, emptiness, withdrawal, and uncontrollable crying episodes. It was a trying period, but she stabilized and moved forward.

Now, here she was a third time, kicking up dust in her own face. Was she to blame this time? Or, was the inevitable happening? She would never know, because she wasn't given a chance to find out. It could have been a combination. But Farren would put the blame on the victimizers—Nakea and Shonda. Each of the concerned parties was ignorant to what transpired, and hoped that Farren would help them out with the answer.

The bright, shining examination room light shimmered, penetrating on Nasir as Farren lifted up and yelled, "It's all his fault! It was his son's mother and her sister!" Nasir backed to the door and palmed his face. Nakea's plan was to retaliate. That's why she pressed charges first. So it could appear to be in self-defense if this was ever taken to court.

"I want you out of here!" Farren words boomed and her body hardened.

Doctor Wayne placed a hand on Nasir's shoulder. "It may be wise to let her deal with her folks alone, with the initial shock of losing a baby. In a few hours, she'll be admitted. But first, we need to perform an exploratory exam to find out how much damage was done to her ovary. She'll be given a sedative to calm her." He patted Nasir again. "Relax, grab a bite to eat and come back later to see her. I've gone through this with hundreds of patients; one in five pregnant women miscarry. She'll be all right in time."

He tried to encourage Nasir with his calm demeanor. It eased him a bit, but Leslie and Raymond were fuming. They wanted to immediately find Nakea and Shonda and have them prosecuted.

In a stern voice, Raymond scolded Farren, "We told you to be very selective when choosing a mate. You asked us to stay out your business—we did! And now, we're—well, I'm, adding my two cents! From the time you told us his father passed and his mother spent time in jail, I knew this relationship was headed for destruction!"

"Now, Raymond! Don't you see our baby hurting? Can't your verbal reprimand wait?"

"No Les, it has to be dealt with now! This boy is to blame! What does he know about a family, when he comes from a broken home? They are mismatched! He's nothing but one of those thugs, unworthy of being with our daughter!"

"Raymond!" Leslie demanded he stopped. "This is unacceptable behavior and I'm asking you to stop, for the sake of Farren. You can chastise *that boy* in the reception area!"

Raymond bumped into Nasir leaving out of the room to get some coffee; ready to yoke him up for hurting his baby girl.

Nasir felt unwelcome and left a few moments after Raymond. The walk through the hallway was a long one for him.

David had begun to fight with the magazines on the tabletop in the waiting room. When Nasir was within distance, he zoomed toward him. "How is she?" His face was riddled with concern. "I tried to help, but they were just beating on her as Farren cried out for her life."

"Was anybody else with them?"

"No, it was only the two of them. I recognized the one young lady. I can point her out. You know we've had problems with her in the past. Hold on." His right eye strained to see as he fought to remember the scene. "There was another guy that came over. I'm not sure if he wanted to help, or if he was there to do more damage. He was driving a Cadillac Seville."

Nasir dug into his left ear; it was itching immensely. He learned from Mom Flossy that meant someone was talking evil about him.

When was this bullshit going to end?

*I'm concentrating so much I don't know
what I'm doing half the time.*
Mark Kaylor

Who Left The Gate Open?

"C'mon, B-right; let me get it for eighty dollars. I got a white dude in the car named Mitch, ready to spend all day long with you if you work wit' me." Bucky was in serious negotiation, but Brian wanted to see the money first. Nasir and Brian had made a pact that he wasn't to sell product to any of Nasir's family members. Including the black sheep of the family— Uncle Bucky. But Bucky had a constant flow of customers coming through, and the money began to stretch long.

Snuffing his life from drugs to rehab to more drugs and less rehab, Bucky was the epitome of a career drug addict.

"Check it . . . I got the money right here." Bucky dug into his pockets pulling out a flap of twenty-dollar bills, equaling to eighty dollars. "I told you—I ain't jivin' you! All I'm asking for you to do is break me off a piece, separately, so I can give this guy his shit. It's a win-win, B-right."

"Gimme the money, ma'fucka. You always runnin' game."

Bucky's left foot shifted behind his right as if he was ready to take off like a competitor in a marathon race. "You know me baby-bee. I got dis all day long.

97

We gon' work together. It's you and me, B-right. We gon' get dis money." Sweat was pouring down his face. Not from the long shirt he had on in the summer time, covering up his track marks, or the jeans he hand on; it was from getting his strip off. He felt like he scored big. He gained the job of being a toter all day, which meant—free get high!

"That's why I call you B-right, 'cause you *be right* with that cook up." Bucky geeked.

"You keep bringing 'em and I got you all night," Brian motivated him to bring him more sales.

"'Ey, nephew been 'round here?"

"Nah, he's working now."

"Yeah, you tell 'em his Unc' is proud of him."

"He's your nephew, you tell him." Brian watched as Bucky slipped away. He zoomed toward the car—a station wagon where a white man, already beamed up, waited to get his next blast.

Brian counted his money, counting over $5,500. It was time to make a drop.

Sean had been watching from a distance, frustrated with himself because he wasn't getting money like niggas on the corner were. From the way Nakea was acting, his first thought was with him being broke; she'd cheat on him again. He had to get money to stop her. That was his logic of it. She was used to him spoiling her, and he found pride in doing so. Now, he couldn't afford to buy a loaf of bread, some bologna or cheese to go with it, to make a sandwich. Nakea was the one footing the bills using her earnings from her job at the warehouse. When he did come up with money, it was borrowed.

As soon as Brian jumped into his hoop ride, Sean was trailing him in a borrowed car. Today he would prove to Chauncey that he was down for his. He reached over to his black duffel bag to make sure his ski mask and gloves were in there. Tucked under the seat was a 9mm that Chauncey threw his way for the job. He wanted some serious arsenal but the 9mm would do the trick. Any piece of steel was better than, not having any at all. Besides, the sun had finally set. When nightfall hit, darkness perpetuated the imagination.

Brian crept quickly into a single car garage on the tree-lined street in his neighborhood. He checked his rear and side view mirror before stepping out his car. His nest was in the tuck, but only a quick ride away from the city. When business started moving for him, he took advantage of it before he got nabbed to buy a house in the quiet, unsuspected suburbs. He knew sooner or later something might occur, and he would be forced to leave the streets. He was smarter than most hustlers though; even outsmarting Nasir. Knowing that a woman was a man's quickest downfall, and he had too much to lose to let one sidetrack him like Nasir had.

Brian was a loner. He lived most of his life in foster care. Although he wasn't abused physically, mentally, he was fucked up behind a woman. Being heavenly endowed, at sixteen, Grace, the foster mother of the house, wanted the other girls in the home to know what it felt like to be with a "man." She had no regard for their welfare. Most of the girls, she treated like sisters, not as a guardian. Yet, Brian, was not a man; he was a teen with a very large penis. Any other young man would die to have been in his position. But for him, it was mental murder. The foster house became chaotic; Grace began disputing and bickering over who would lay with him at night. Rules? There were none! This housemother was in it for what she could get out of it—some custodial care cash and having sex with minors!

Tired of being used, Brian threatened to contact the State if they didn't stop treating him like a tossed football—whoever caught the pass, scored for the night. The request was granted, and from then on, Brian would only have sex with females of his choice.

Later, when life on the block helped his finances, he rented an apartment jointly with Nasir and purchased himself a home. Learning early that a woman is a man's quickest downfall, Brian put them to the side to get that dough—the chicks would always be there!

Nasir found it hilarious about Brian's past, when he shared with him, his darkest secret.

"Yo, you was hittin' old moms Grace?"

"Word! I threw up every time after I hit it too; it was nasty. I don't see how you keep hittin' old ass Lena off."

"'Cause the old heads pussy is blazin', that's why. She's a freak-a-leak," he admitted.

"Yeah, but she's also a child molester—on the real! How old was you when you first hit?"

"I was damn near grown—seventeen."

"Still, she's old enough to be your mother. I was fourteen when Grace started coming in my room, and sixteen, when I started hittin' off all the other females in the house."

"Yo, I would've loved that! One big ass orgy and I'm the only dude slayin' . . . *shiiit*! I wish it was me!"

"I wish it were you too, then you'd know how that shit fucks with you."

"It would fuck wit' me a'ight—all up in here." He grabbed his crotch and both of them laughed. "My game would be top rank! Nigga, and you cryin'—man up and stop sittin' sideways!"

"A'ight. Laugh now cry later . . . don't let a bitch bring you down!"

Brian had more pussy than some men did in a lifetime before he turned sixteen. He was all too familiar with Nasir's situation with his women problems. But he charged that to his boy's hot head— two of them; one of them on his shoulders and the other, between his legs—that kept his ass in hot water. He was a no-nonsense man. He didn't take shit from them broads. That's why when it came to them, it was fuck them and leave them—that was it. He wasn't about getting hit by the bow and arrow. He was about twisting the bow out, not getting stuck by it.

Sean's creep ride was parked two blocks away, patiently waiting for Brian to come into view. When Brian exited his car, Sean was slithering beside other cars to shield himself, hoping nosy neighbors were too busy doing other things to notice him.

His sixth sense caused Brian to turn around, but by this time, Sean had the knock on him.

"Bitch, don't say a word. You know what it is! Run it fucka!" Holding his lips tightly, Brian thought about challenging him, but the steel that was shoved in the nape of his neck, pushed him from any possible view the neighbors may have had, back into the darkness of the garage, and told him don't try to be a tough guy, just hand what he had over.

"What the fuck is taking you so long?"

"Mafucka, the gun in my neck. How the fuck you expect me to give you something with my hands above my head?"

"Oh, you wanna be a smart nigga. You better shut the fuck up, pussy, before I drop two in you!" With one hand on the gun, with his free hand, Sean explored Brian's pockets.

"What, you a gay nigga? Feelin' all on my dick." Antagonizing his robber was his tactic to take him out of his zone.

"Suck my dick, you bitch ass nigga!" Instead of throwing him off, Brian made Sean angrier. Courtesy of the privacy of Brian's garage, Sean took the butt of the gun and smashed the fuck out of Brian's head. Then stripped him of his cash, his backpack with four ounces in it, and yanked off his jewels around his neck. He left Brian dizzy on the steps and fled to his creep ride to getaway.

When Brian came to, he had a strenuous headache and a huge knot on his head with blood still tricking down from it. Privately, he recaptured the robbery. The assailant had to follow him home. This meant he knew where he slept. Not too many people knew of this spot.

Brian staggered inside the house to the bathroom, and saw that blood was seeping from his head down his neck, staining his blue T-shirt. It was possible that he needed a stitch or two. Brian reached in his cabinet and pulled out a bottle of Tylenol. Popping two pills in his mouth, he cupped his hand and filled it with faucet water, raised it to his mouth and took a sip to down the pills.

Opening the linen closet, he reached for a dark colored towel to throw around his neck to soak up the dripping blood. He then went into his bedroom closet and took out a red Francois Girbaud shirt to replace the soiled shirt he had on. After he changed, he dialed Nasir's number to tell him about the attack, on his ride to the hospital.

"Yo"

"What up, B?" Nasir was back at the apartment sorting out shit; wondering how he should deal with Nakea and Shonda. He'd picked up Li'l Marv from Mrs. Lois' house and put him to bed; staring at him as he lay in his crib, taking nothing else into account. Why did his son have to grow up with a mother like Nakea?

"Yo, I got stuck. A nigga followed me home and vicked me."

Nasir shouted, "Damn, B!" As if he hadn't been through enough today. "How many dudes was it?"

"Just one, but I wasn't strapped."

"Fuck, nigga! You know the rules: always carry your shit!"

"The block was too hot to keep my piece on me. I had my shit at Tyra's house. I needed to make a drop real quick, so I left my shit there not thinking."

"Did you see the dude?"

"Nah, he had on a black ski mask."

"What he get you for?"

"I had four ounces on me and five thousand five hundred dollars cash. Yo, the nigga even snatched my chain with the 'One Love' charm on it!"

"That's fucked up, but he really didn't come off with much, so count that as a blessing. And whoever it was, fucked up when he took that chain. That shit will appear on the streets. We'll find out who it was."

"True dat. I gotta nice knot on my shit. Nigga pounded me in the head. I'm about to go to the emergency room to get this shit stitched up."

"The hospital . . ." Nasir sighed. "Yo, I told you that Farren was pregnant, right?"

"Nah. Should I say congrats?"

"Nah, man, she had a miscarriage today. Nakea and Shonda jumped her. She was already at risk of losing the baby. They beat the dog mess outta her. She don't want to see me 'bout nothing right now."

"Damn! Nakea still doing stupid shit, huh? You still running in that?"

"Hell no! I been stop fuckin' wit' that ho."

"Yo, I'ma hit you back. I'm at the hospital."

"A'ight."

Love that is not madness is not love.

Pedro Calderon de la Barca

Sick Wit' It

Sean made off with a quick $5,500, four ounces of cocaine, a necklace and a charm that read: ONE LOVE. The four ounces he would sell for seven hundred an ounce and make $2,800. Easy money—free money to him. Add that to the cash, and Sean came off with $8,300. That was enough to get him back on his feet. Deducting from that would be a used car, and a bedroom set for him and Nakea. He was tired on sleeping on a mattress without a bed frame. He'd hit the stores for a few 'fits, and with the rest of the money, jumpstart his hustle.

Nakea was lying on the mattress in their bedroom which was barely furnished. Their furnishings consisted of a portable radio with a CD player, and five blue plastic totes, full of clothes. There was only one picture hanging on the wall that was hung with a pushpin and that was of Li'l Marv.

Sean was in the living room sitting on the worn brown sofa that was donated to Nakea by the Catholic charities, with the money and coke laid out on the table in front of him. He got up to peep in both bedrooms. Nakea was asleep and Shonda wasn't home. He figured she was out getting her ass wet up—

dragging her baby girl along in the process. Going back into the living room, he placed the call to Chauncey to let him know the job was done.

"I did that," Sean confirmed triumphantly to him.

"Did you come off, kid?" He didn't want any of the proceeds. What Sean came off with, was all his.

"Four O's and a li'l cash. Nothing to brag about, but it's a come up."

"You straight? Meet me tomorrow and we can get this thing poppin'. Get money, nigga!"

"Get money," Sean repeated with force.

"Yo, I seen your girl today too."

"Word? Where at?" Sean inquired with his indicators flashing.

"She was at Nasir's girl's job. Her and her sister was beatin' the shit out the girl."

"For real?"

"No bullshit. Me, and that ho, Sonya, saw that shit. That girl gotta be fucked up. They whipped her ass over that nigga," Chauncey instigated.

"Mmmm," Sean hummed. "I'll get with you tomorrow, kid."

"One."

Sean snatched up the cocaine, tucking it away. He put the money inside a shoebox and stormed into the room to wake Nakea up.

"Get ya monkey ass up!" He jerked a handful of her hair to get her to her feet. Nakea stumbled to her feet with crust in her eyes and blurred vision, whining, "What's wrong with you?"

From the shrill in Sean's voice, she knew a fight was stemming.

"Where the fuck was you at today?"

"I was with Shonda, why?" She grabbed his hand to stop him from pulling out her weave.

"Bitch, *don't lie* to me."

"I'm not! I was with Shonda!"

"What the fuck was you doing at Nasir's girl's job?"

"Handling my mothafuckin' business. Now let my hair go!" she insisted.

Sean let her hair go, but yanked her head down so hard, her body fell back. He leaped on her and started punching her in the face. Nakea swung back, digging into his skin with her nails, breaking his skin. He got off of her and collared her up by her long white night shirt.

"Bring ya foul ass in here!" He dragged her inside the bathroom and mashed her face against the medicine cabinet mirror. "See this man?" One of her eyes was squashed against the mirror. With one eye, she looked back and saw a madman.

"This is the man that will kill yo' ass or have ya ass bodied! Am I making myself clear?" Hauling her back into the bedroom, he told her to strip naked.

Nakea was weeping. "Are you fucking crazy?"

"You ain't seen crazy yet, but you will if you don't do what I told you to do!" She removed her nightshirt and her panties. "What did you have on today?"

Nakea turned toward a corner in the room. "Those clothes in the dirty clothes pile right there."

"Get 'em." He shoved her.

She walked ass naked over to get them, and handed them to him. He searched the clothes over and pulled out the underwear that were stuffed inside her shorts. He unraveled them, inspecting the crusty white discharge in the crotch and threw them in her face.

"You fucked the nigga, didn't you?"

Nakea threw her hands over her face to protect herself. "I didn't fuck anybody," she screamed.

"You think I'm stupid, bitch?"

"No, Sean, but I didn't fuck nobody. That's the truth!"

"You lying, bitch! It's cum in those panties."

"That's not cum, Sean—it's discharge—all women discharge!" she tried to explain. But he wasn't hearing that.

"Bitch, you's a liar!" He hurried to the living room and went to the spot where he hid his gun. He

KASHAMBA WILLIAMS

retrieved it and turned to go back in the room with the gun cocked. "Did you fuck dat nigga, Kee?"

When Nakea looked at what she created, she couldn't believe she'd made a bigger mess by getting back with Sean—a mess that she didn't know how to clean up.

"*No Sean!* Please don't do this . . . I didn't fuck nobody," she cried for dear life.

"Lay down on the mattress." He demanded her, and put the gun to his side. Nakea dropped down and lay back. "Open ya legs!" He kicked one of her legs open to spread them wide. He knelt down and smothered her pussy with his nose to smell it. Then he ascended back, removed his shorts and came out of his boxers to mount her. He forced his dick inside of her aggressively to make sure her pussy was tight. After a few hard strokes and he backed off of her.

"You better be glad the pussy ain't tampered with. Put ya night shirt back on."

What he did wasn't about pleasure. He wanted to feel inside her walls to find out if another man had been in there. Nakea put her panties and nightshirt back on. Sean watched every movement she made.

"Why you fucking with his bitch?" Sean's back rested against the door with his finger on the trigger of the 9mm. But this time it wasn't pointed at her; it was being waved in the air. One careless move of his trigger

112

finger, and a bullet would rip through the wall or land in Nakea's body.

"She had it coming to her. It wasn't about him— She attempted to convince Sean as she wiped her red eyes.

"Kee, I will take you out if I find out anything different. Now go back to sleep. It's late." He turned off the light and went back into the living room to catch the late night episodes of the "Dave Chappell Show."

911 Is a Joke!

Two days later, home from the hospital, Farren was on the phone bitching to the police department.

"How can that be?" commented Farren, who was in disbelief that she had to turn herself in because of the warrant Nakea had issued. She had called to find out what she needed to do to have a warrant taken out on Nakea for assault, when they were told her she had to turn herself in.

"Ma'am, I can only tell you what I know. You have a warrant out for your arrest. Until you resolve this matter, no, you can not sign a warrant out on another individual," the officer on the receiving end stated the facts to her.

"You mean to tell me that I was victimized by this woman and I can't file a complaint on her? I lost my baby! Do you understand what I am telling you? And you are telling *me* to turn *myself* in, and deal with this bogus warrant? How fucked up is that?"

"Wait a minute now," the officer interjected, "do you realize how many complaints we would have if we allowed people who have been in altercations with each other, to sign warrants on one another? Our office would be full with thousands of time consuming cases. First come, first served!"

"That's your job, ain't it? You get paid to protect and serve, right?"

"From our records, Ms. Giles, you attacked this woman first. If it's not true, fight your case in court. But I advise you to hang up this phone and turn yourself in, before detectives show up at your house, or better yet, your job, with handcuffs. Save the embarrassment of being taken away, especially, if it's in front of your employer.

"Fine!" Farren threw the cordless phone across the room, shattering it. Nasir came through the door with Li'l Marv. Farren stared him down without a word, then stomped off to the bedroom and slammed the door, shaking the wall. She didn't want to see Nasir or Li'l Marv. Actually, she wanted them to turn right back around, and let her be. Nasir wanted to share the news with her that while she was in the hospital, the owner of the three-bedroom house they inspected had approved their rental application.

Removing his son from his arms to the walker, Li'l Marv smiled, showing his gums to his daddy. Nasir walked back to talk with Farren only to find out the bedroom door was locked. Twisting the knob, he pounded on the door. While at the hospital Farren hadn't accepted his calls, and had turned him away for the past two days.

"Open the door, Farren. We can't go on like this. Haven't we been through enough?"

"Go to hell, Nasir! Just leave—just go, and take your son with you!" Her freedom of speech revealed her combination of pain and suffering. Yet, the baby's involvement wasn't warranted in her grief. If she didn't want Nasir around that was one issue, but the baby, that was taking it to another level. However, Nasir was far from persuading her to let him off this easy, even with his ill feelings.

"Farren, open the door!"

"Go away, Nasir!"

"I'm not going anywhere until you talk to me."

"I'm not opening the door." She wouldn't budge from the bed as she curled up with two thick pillows, noticing Nasir had finally cleaned the bleeding heart off the mirror. She still hadn't had a chance to call Dennis and find out the names of those he showed the house to. She decided it was too late; he'd probably forgotten since days had passed.

"Do you want me to kick it in? 'Cause I will."

"I've been through enough violence, but if that's what you want to do, go ahead!"

Nasir stood close to the door, talking through the cracks. "I've got good news," he said, trying to force the knob to unlock with pressure.

"So!"

"We were approved to rent the house you begged me to go see."

"It doesn't matter. I'm not moving anywhere—you can! This is where I'll be. I'm calling Dennis to rescind the lease termination letter."

Nasir had finally applied enough pressure to disengage the lock. Farren's face was puffy and her eyelids were heavy from expressing her sadness. Nasir went to touch her. Farren scrambled to the other side of the bed like an abused child, trying to get away.

"You helped them kill my baby," she squealed at the top of her voice, picking up an object near her, throwing it at him.

Nasir swiftly moved to evade being the target. "I'ma let you cool down for a few days and give you some space. Your conversation, and the way you are acting is beginning to turn me off!" His voice matched hers.

"See you!" she ushered out her mouth, standing up for confrontation.

Nasir gathered a basket of clothes to take with him. He had items of clothing at his tuck crib, but not enough for the length of time he planned on being there. He also scooped up clothes for Li'l Marv and threw a few extra bottles and pampers in the basket, leaving Farren alone to sit in her misery.

For a moment, Farren flatly stared, and then with dignity straightened herself up, until she heard the door close as they left. She stayed in the room to make sure they were gone. Momentarily, she came out the room, relieved that Nasir took her advice and left. All these complexities lay ahead for them. To clear herself of one, she was prepared to face the Division of Public Safety.

The radio in Farren's new Infiniti G20, courtesy of her parents, murmured with a smooth melody; a brief interruption, but soothing to her ears. When she arrived at the police station, she couldn't dodge the pain that she felt from her miscarriage. But this had to be handled before she'd suffer another form of embarrassment publicly—getting locked up. Greeted with roars of laughter and loud talk, mostly smothered by gargled chatter, Farren made her way to the bulletproof window with a small circle opening for her to speak into.

"Yes, my name is Farren Giles, and I'm here to turn myself in." Farren made sure she wore an extra absorbent overnight maxi-pad in case she was there over four hours. The bleeding wasn't very heavy, but it was a steady flow. In her purse were four backup pads.

AT THE COURT'S MERCY

Officer Salvati came from behind the guarded area and escorted Farren to the booking area. His blue, *protect and serve* uniform perfectly fit the mold of his contour. For a spaghetti eating, garlic loving, tomato sauce smelling Italian, Salvati was evenly tanned, with jet-black shoulder length hair that could easily be pulled back in a ponytail. He was an Italian beauty but his attitude stank, which made him ugly all over.

After seating Farren in the criminal's chair for booking, Officer Salvati keyed her name in their database and printed out the warrant. He read off the charges to her as though she was a waste of his time, and commenced to take her through the booking process.

"How can I counter file against the *victim*?" Farren asked with raised sarcasm in her voice.

"Ms. Giles, would you stand over there and place your index finger on the ink pad?" He didn't give a damn about her concerns. His job was booking, and that is what he planned to do—book her.

The moulie could save all her questions for a detective that would listen to her explain her side of the story, he thought.

Farren placed her index finger on the ink pad and Officer Salvati used his hand to apply pressure on her finger for the ink to absorb in a half-shaped circular motion.

"Place your finger on the fingerprint card located on your right," he ordered, going directly by the books.

The fingerprint card was a few spaces away.

Farren moved to where it was and placed her fingerprint on it thinking, *I can't believe I'm being arrested. I'll have a criminal record behind this girl playing games. All the shit I let that girl slide with when she was doing petty shit, and now, I'm the one that has to plead my side of the case in court? I may have behaved irrationally when I busted out her eardrum, but she's done worse—I loss my baby behind her.*

The aching to cry was heavy on the inside, and she struggled to hold back the tears. Maybe the way she was treating Nasir as a result of what happened was wrong; not realizing that he strongly valued her feelings and having a family with her. But her true feelings were suppressed. Losing the baby was the drive to her final decision—Nakea had to pay the ultimate price. If she couldn't counteract with a warrant, she would get her without the help of the law.

An insecure and evil friend is more to be feared than a wild beast; a wild beast may wound your body, but an evil friend will wound your mind.

Buddha

Holla at Cha Boy!

Lena drove her son's Magnum through the city, booming *Turn off the Lights,* an old school jam by Teddy Pendergrass that, back in her day old, playas made babies off of. Heads turned and the young hustlers were checking out the ride: deep-sea blue with sparkling 20's riding the wheels, shitting on all the other cars passing by. Only four hours ago Quinton had the rims put on, and Lena decided to take it for a spin. Riding through the strip where the ballas were known to frequent.

"Yo, who the fuck is that? That shit is hot!" Chauncey admired the Magnum from the stoop. "Is that a bitch in the ride?"

"What is it to you if it is?" Sonya was on her last wind with him. He only kept her around to stir trouble, give him head, and help make him some money. Ride or die chick, she was definitely that.

"Don't live today that you outgrow yesterday, ho! If I hadn't been updating your ass, you'd be still chasing behind sucker ass Nasir." That instantly shut her up.

Lena slowly approached the corner. She could see why the young girls had a hard time keeping their legs closed. There were so many fine ass young tenders, flexing muscle and large dick prints, for them to choose from.

"Yo." Chauncey leaned forward to see inside the car. "Pull that joint over." He whistled, then, called her to get his swerve on. Lena could see him waving at her from the street. She hit the automatic window release to lower the passenger's side window.

"Are you waving to me?"

Chauncey excused himself and made it to the car; leaning inside to survey Lena's goods, feeling the slow groove of Teddy.

"Damn, old moms, what you doin' swervin' in this shit?"

Lena dropped her shoulders. "Old moms? No, baby, this is seasoned meat right here, that's all."

Chauncey smiled at her sassiness. "What you doin' 'round here? You ain't here to cop are you?"

"Only if you're selling a little weed." She used her thumb and her index finger to imitate her smoking a joint. "Other than that, hell no. I ain't looking for nothing else."

"Nothing at all? How about a strong back to dig you out? With ya fine, seasoned ass."

"I'm flattered, but I have a son your age. I don't make it my business to deal with little boys."

"What that gotta do with me?" Like every young hustler, Chauncey had to have an old mom to hit off every once in awhile.

Lena examined his contents. He had to be some years older than Nasir, but was he worth her time? Her affair with Nasir was about vengeance, but this one would be about pleasure.

"Jot this number down, and call me later."

"Is this trash or should I treasure this?" he questioned, holding up the piece of paper he'd written her number down on.

"Depending on what you want me to be."

Chauncey stepped back, biting the corner of his upper lip. "Say no more."

"Except—" Lena cut her eyes. "Your name?"

"Chauncey."

"Okay, Chauncey, I'm—"

"Your old moms," he finished off her name, as if he wanted to remember it and know her. "I'll get up with you later." He turned his back to her, walking back up the street to un-poke Sonya's lips.

"What was that all about?" Sonya asked, swinging her feet from the stoop.

"Anybody ever tell you, you ask too many damn questions?" The conversation between them was empty. Other than having sex, getting money, and her helping him bring Nasir down, they didn't have anything more in common.

Without saying anything to him, Sonya walked off. She was growing tired of being disrespected by her so-called partners. Strutting and trailing past the park, she held her head in dignity. The word "ho" had become an extension to her name, and those in her surroundings used it without conviction. Even if Sonya wanted to turn her life around, she would still be known as Sonya, the ho. So, why change? Be the best damn ho—the number one ho, second to none. And if leaving men alone who weren't down for who she was is what she had to do, the hell with them. If necessary, ditching Chauncey if she had to, then she'd do so. Before she did that, she had a few tricks up her sleeve.

Unlocking the door to her mother's house Sonya found her mother, Marie, and her Aunt Mitzy, sitting at the kitchen table, reminiscing. Classic jams were playing on the "Grown and Sexy" radio dial.

"Remember this shit, Marie?" Mitzy was half full of E&J Brandy, liquor that made women grow chest hair, doing an impression of the bop dance without a partner. "I would fuck this dance up," She partied, inviting her niece to join them. "Hey, niecey, c'mon have a sip with me and your mom."

Sonya sat in the chair next to her mother; days like this were habitual since Marie was laid off of work—

home relaxing, collecting unemployment. Marie fell out in laughter, reaching to give Sonya a cocktail glass half filled with ice. "Here, pour your own. I don't wanna give you too much if you can't handle it."

"Pour me to the top, I need to lift my mood. But hit me off with that Remy Red, not that gasoline," she said to her mom, referring to the E&J.

"What's wrong, niecey? Cute as you are, you should be tearing away from all these fine young boys around here. Whatever came about between you and Marv Bundy's son?

"Who Nasir?"

"Yeah, Loretta's boy. You know her ass ain't been the same since Marv died, and she did eighteen years for that nigga. That fucked her up!"

Marie smiled in memory of Marv Sr. "Well, if Nasir is anything like his daddy, he's one hella man!"

"I'll drink to that." Mitzy situated her glass in the air and all of them touched glasses.

"I don't mess with him like I used to. He got a woman." Sonya made it seem like they were really a couple before, when really, she was only an easy lay to him.

"His father kept a woman, but that didn't stop him none. Mitzy, you recall that time when you guided Loretta to the motel and that crazy bitch got in the bed with me and Marv after he finished rocking my world, and I was naked?"

Mitzy spit out her drink from laughing so hard. Sonya was surprised. "Mom, I didn't know you messed around with Nasir's dad!"

"Chile, that's old news. Marv was the sharpest black piece of specimen in our day. All the women wanted him, and I was lucky enough to have had him while he was on this earth. I will never forget that man. Damn shame what happened to him."

"He did leave an impact like that," Mitzy agreed. "If Bucky wasn't on that shit like that, Marv probably would be alive."

"Who's Bucky?" Sonya inquired.

"Shit, that old dope head. You see him coming through the block to cop. You just don't know him; he's Nasir's uncle, his mother's brother. He's the reason Marv is dead today, fucking with the dope game."

"You right about that; Marv beat Bucky's ass over that shit, but Freeze put a knife in him. Stabbed him up terrible; killing the man." Mitzy recalled. "That's why I only sippy-sip my liquor. Drugs have you fucked up. You either end up in jail, strung out, or dead over that shit. Alcohol ain't never killed nobody; except when people drink and drive," she scrutinized.

"For his sake, I hope his son isn't following in his footsteps." Marie aimed at her daughter.

"I see him out there getting his mack on. If I was his age, I'd fuck him with quickness," Mitzy slyly snickered.

"I guess Nasir does take after his father then, 'cause he does have his way with the ladies and the dope game." Sonya now had a better perception of why Nasir *was* the way he was—it was in his genes.

"Nasir ain't Marv's only son. He's got that other boy by Lena." Mitzy looked to Marie for the boy's name. "Eer, what's her son's name?"

"It's Quinton. How can you forget that? That damn Lena had to announce it to every damn body. Marv ain't never deny that he was his son, so he must be."

"I only knew Nasir to have one sister. Is Quinton older or younger than him?" This was new news to Shonda, and she tried to figure out if she knew him.

"Older, Nasir was an infant when Marv died. Quinton had to be six or seven months, something like that," Marie concluded.

"Quinton huh . . . I got to investigate that." Sonya was curious to find out. "Mom, top me off one more time, before I get dressed and join the nightlife.

"You better be careful out there. It's not like when we were coming up," she gave her fair warning. They had an open relationship and Sonya didn't hold back when it came to talking with her mother.

It was about 11 p.m. when Chauncey pulled out his cell phone to hook up with Lena. Encouraged by her willingness to flirt, he wanted her to answer for a late night date.

"This is Lena."

"Old moms, can I get at you?"

Lena was oiling down her legs from a refreshing bubble bath. "No need to play games, Chauncey. I'd appreciate if you were straight up with me."

With his hands behind his head, elbows pointing outward, he admired her forwardness. "I like a woman who knows what she wants."

"Now you're talking my language." One leg was peaked high in the air as she rubbed the oil in circular motion with pleasure on the mind.

"Where's your man?"

"What's it matter to you?"

Focusing on her expectations of him, Chauncey got his reply. "I see, no date, no dinner, strictly fucking, huh?"

"That's all it could ever be. What can a young man really do for me, other than give me a stiff dick?"

"Nothing. I'm glad that's clear. So, when can we meet up?"

There was contemplation from Lena.

"Come now, 708 Washington Street."

Quinton was out for the night, working the late-night shift, and not expected to return until morning. Lena knew Nasir would never come unannounced. Besides, it only went down when he called.

"Give me twenty minutes, I'll be there." Chauncey seized five lubed condoms and one mint flavored condom, and put them in his back pocket for an all night session. That's how long he planned to bang it out.

Forgiveness is the final form of love.

Reinhold Niebuhr

Busted

Li'l Marv was irritable, restless and crying. Nasir, inexperienced with teething babies, could not get him to sleep. And he had plans for the evening. He called his mother to ask if she would mind babysitting, but she told him, "I don't baby-sit for parents to run the streets and trick. Stay home with your son." With no luck there, he tried warming up milk to soothe him— that didn't work. He tried rocking him in his arms— that didn't work. He tried walking him back and forth—that didn't work. The only other person, other than Nakea, that could calm him was Farren. But she was going through changes. At this point, he took his chance and called her. Farren didn't answer the phone and let the answering machine respond.

"Farren, pick up, I really need you." Li'l Marv was crying in the background. "I can't get Marv to sleep. It's probably this strange motel room. You know he ain't used to sleeping in these shits," he lied to protect his hideaway. "Are you there? Answer, please. Do you mind if I bring him home, then pick him up in the morning? You hear the baby in the background. Pick up the phone."

AT THE COURT'S MERCY

Farren tried to ignore Nasir, but the cries of the baby wrestled with her emotions. *Why won't he call Nakea? It's her baby! Should I do this?* She pondered. *All right,* she picked up the receiver and the answer machine beeped to stop recording. "Bring him over and don't think about staying!"

∞∞∞∞∞∞

It was 3 a.m., and now Nasir couldn't sleep. The same bullshit that tormented him for months was continually causing his pressure to rise. *How in the hell did it arrive to this point?* The whispers in his ear were familiar words. Initially, he paid no attention to them.

"Was the pussy good to you?"

After Nasir dropped Li'l Marv off, he took a ride to get his little hottie, Shanira, from the projects. He was wrong for that, but Farren wasn't in a position to give him some, and Lena, oddly enough, hadn't answered his call. He didn't know what was up with that; she never missed his calls. Anyway, he wanted to see what Shanira could make her bottom lips do.

Shanira cleared her throat and turned her body to cuddle with his.

"Yeah, it was proper."

"How come you ain't sleep then? Good pussy will knock a nigga out. You ain't sleep. That's an insult to me. I guess I didn't do a good job. How about another round?" She used her tongue and ran it across his neck.

"Don't." He stopped her, but she continued. This time she licked slower and closer to his earlobe.

"Why? My pussy is still tingling for you."

Nasir put his head back and let Shanira take full advantage of his body. This was the first night that he'd stayed away from Farren. She had been blowing up his cell phone an hour after he dropped off his son, so he turned his phone off.

Using their last episode, the fighting and disrespect in front of his son, to justify his cheating. Being faithful was a hard task when sex was his addiction. It had nothing to do with love. It was the power of having any woman he desired. He had yet to find one who turned him down.

Even the most highly-respectable teachers at Charter Elementary were throwing themselves at him. But how many strange punannies could he indulge in, before he dipped inside a bad dose? It's amazing what a woman would do when she thought a man had money to help her advance. And from the way Nasir carried himself: his clean cut, tie and slacks, fronting for the school, then, when in his hood, his pants sagged and his white tees were bright. Adapting like a chameleon, he had them fooled in both worlds.

In the morning he had to return home to get his son. Being a father was more than just being called "Daddy" to him. He spent time to nourish and provide for his namesake. There wasn't anything like a father's love, but he highly praised a mother's love.

Nakea had that love for her son and he credited her for that. He thought Farren did too. But was hers a phony mask that embraced step-motherhood? Or, as tree leaves that gravely await death; did Farren's "mother role" for another woman's child, die too? Li'l Marv was the one connection that Nasir had to another woman, and Farren wanted to end that— jealousy overcame her.

Have You Seen Him?

Farren's black posh Aéropostale slip-ons made sliding noises as she marched back and forth from the bedroom to the bathroom. There was no way she could have made Nasir *that* mad, that he didn't want to deal with her now. She had some "choice" words for him, but he was being petty by letting his voicemail pick up on the first ring.

Where the hell is he? Farren's worrying turned into ranting and raving.

At first, she thought he'd made a pit-stop to kick it with Brian, but after she phoned him and he gave her the run around, she knew that wasn't so.

Then, she thought the worst. *Maybe he was in a car accident after he left here, and can't call me back!*

She dialed all the local hospitals, checking to see if they had a Marvin Bundy, Jr. listed as a patient—no hit. Worried, she dialed Loretta's number, with the likelihood that he was there. She'd already called Mom Flossy's, awakening her out of her sleep; she told her, she hadn't seen him.

It was five in the morning and Farren was still on her quest to reach Nasir. Loretta was out cold. Not just from sleep, but also from the ice-cold air conditioner that was placed in her bedroom window, that blew directly on her body. The phone had to ring about six times before Loretta picked it up.

"Who is it?" she asked groggily.

"Um, hi, Ms. Loretta. This is Farren, um . . ."

From her experience with dealing with a cheating man, Loretta knew why Farren was calling at this time of morning. "He ain't here!"

"Well, have you heard from him?"

"Listen, don't try to pry information from me; he's *your* man! I don't keep a tab on him, *you* do."

Farren remained calm, "Please, Ms. Loretta, he may be in trouble. I've been trying to reach him."

Loretta let her take a breather. "Maybe he don't wanna talk, or else he'd call you back. Now, I heard you had an incident, shouldn't you be resting?"

"If Nasir comes or calls, please tell him to call home." Farren didn't want to get indignant with her because she was still Nasir's mother, and she was taught to be polite to her elders.

"Wait!" Loretta said energized. "Ride through Seventh and Washington, you'll probably find him over there." She lay back on her pillow, closed her eyes and smiled.

Let's see how you handle that, Miss Farren!

Here was the chance to put an end to this relationship.

Farren went back into the bedroom and covered up Li'l Marv, making sure he was still asleep. She threw on a pair of Nike shorts, a halter top, and some Airforce Ones. She brushed her hair back in a ponytail as she did back in her basketball days, then rushed to get to 7th & Washington Street.

Why is he over that way? I'm telling you, if he's back hustling, I'm really done. That's why he dropped Li'l Marv off, lying bastard! What other reason would he be over there?

She skidded corners, thinking how Nasir plotted. It took her fifteen minutes to get to the west side of town. Her car came to a halt behind Quinton's new Magnum, that she didn't know he had. While she knew Lena lived on the same block of Washington Street, it didn't dawn on her that her house was the house Loretta was referring to.

Pulling her keys from the ignition, Farren stepped out of her car and proceeded to walk down the block to check and see if Nasir was out there. This early in the morning it was scarce, most people were inside. She walked down two blocks, then, came back around.

I must be losing my mind! This man me got out here five twenty in the morning, searching for his ass. Let me take my bee-hind home.

She was so angry with him, and when she saw the male figure leaning against her car, she wanted to run to tell him how she felt. However, it wasn't Nasir. It was Quinton, departing from the house to get himself some breakfast, but when he saw the Infiniti G20 he'd seen Farren driving around in parked behind his car, he waited for her. Chauncey had come and gone. Quinton had come home from work a little while ago, and her car wasn't out there. With her car posted up in front of his house, he thought she was coming to see him.

"I knew you'd come back to daddy." He winked at her with his narrow-mind. "That man you have must not be treating you right."

"What are you doing here, Quinton?"

"Nah, that's the question I'm asking you. What are you doing here at *my* house?"

"For your information, I'm passing through."

"Then, why are you posted up behind my shit?"

Farren took a few steps back, "This you?"

"You love this shit don't you? I could put your name on the passenger's seat. It could be Quinton's and Farren's." He tried to gas her.

"Weak!" she spat from his wishful thinking. "Run that game on your baby momma—not me!"

"You *are* one of them. You will always be. You know that."

"Not in my mind, maybe yours."

"Let me get a hug for old-time sake."

Farren utterly yearned to unwind. What's more is that she'd given her heart to Nasir, but Quinton was the love of her life at one point. A little hug was harmless.

"Don't have the time; gotta go. I got too much on my mind."

"Wanna talk it over, over breakfast? I know you hungry with your greedy ass."

"Can't." Farren felt comfort standing in the security of his arms again.

Talking in her ear softly, Quinton asked, "Why not?"

"I have to get going, Q." After she said it, she realized she slipped. Old feelings had surfaced and tricked her into using her pet name for him.

"Damn, I haven't heard you call me that since we last made love . . . Q, you're going too deep, you're hurting me!" he mimicked her.

Farren covered her mouth, glowing, "You didn't go there."

"Yes, we did go there. It wasn't always bad times for us . . . we have a history. Can you say that about young boy?"

"I'll admit it wasn't, but when the bad times came, they wore me down. It's just a bad time for me now. Q, I . . . I—" She tripped over her tongue. "I had another miscarriage."

Quinton pressed forward holding her tight. Farren melted in his arms cozily, with her breasts resting on his chest. He smelled the back of her neck. Farren felt his nose and closed her eyes. Catching herself, she opened her eyes precisely in time to catch sight of Nasir, riding through with a female in the passenger seat of his Lincoln. Both of their eyes locked on each other, growing bigger as they stared. Farren pushed Quinton away and ran to her car to trail them.

"Where are you going?" Quinton called to her. He turned his head to see the back of Nasir's car, and nodded with a shady sneer.

Fuck that young boy! He thought.

Farren ran two red lights trying to catch up to Nasir, but when she came to a commonly used city intersection, she was scared to risk the light, knowing she left Li'l Marv home alone. Her brakes came to a screeching halt as Nasir gained distance from her.

Inside of his car, Nasir was asking for a fight. *What the fuck?* Shanira looked at him at a complete loss, asking, "What's wrong, boo?"

His attitude had switched up. "Shut the fuck up! I'ma let you out right here. Yo, take this two hundred dollars and I'll get back."

When he handed Shanira the bills, she let his cockiness pass. *Shit, that's more than half of my welfare check.* She thought. "Call me boo, *okay?*"

They were in her cousin's neighborhood and she could chill over his house, before finding out what time the next city bus was going to her side of town.

"Yeah, yeah," Nasir mumbled. "I'll get up."

He peeled tires, racing to get around the block; wanting to know what the hell Farren was doing hugged up with Quinton—her ex-man—in front of Lena's house, when she was supposed to be home watching Li'l Marv. His guilt beat him in the head.

Was she knockin' this nigga off all along? Did she let him it hit while she was bleeding?

Knowing that Farren was trying to locate his whereabouts, he retracted and ended up in the rear of her car.

The light had finally changed and Farren policed the street. She saw Nasir flee down. She glanced in her rearview, mirror slamming on brakes after detecting Nasir. His car damn near rear-ended her from his abrupt stop. Farren ascended from the car, as did Nasir; ready to go to war with words.

"What the fuck you doin' with that nigga?" Nasir was in a fit of fury.

Farren pushed his hand out of her face. "Don't even try it! Who the fuck was that in the passenger's seat of your car? You dropped your son off to me to trick? After all the shit I've been through!"

"Fuck what you saw! Where the fuck is my son and what the fuck was you doin' all hugged up with dude?"

Nasir had to know. What if she was there because Lena decided to tell it all, and Quinton was there to act on behalf of the consoler? He quickly dismissed that, figuring if she had, Farren would be much angrier than this, so he focused on seeing her with Quinton.

"I called your mom and she told me I could find you on Seventh and Washington."

"That's some bullshit! She ain't tell you no shit like that."

"She did! Why else would I be over here?"

"It don't take a rocket *mothafuckin'* scientist to figure that out. You creepin' and you got caught!"

"Please, it's been over between me and Q."

"You calling the nigga pet names? Yo, what's up with you?"

"Fuck you, Nasir! This is it with you. You don't give a shit about me; riding around town with bitches in the front seat of your car, like you don't have an ounce of respect for your woman at home who just loss *your* baby!"

"Was it really *my* baby?"

By reaction, Farren slapped his face. "You are full of shit!"

Nasir's nostrils flared just like his father's did when he was taken there. "Answer my questions—where is my son and what is up with you and dude?"

"You really wanna know?"

Nasir gripped Farren's wrist and pushed her against the car. "Do it seem like a fuckin' game to you? I should beat ya ass!"

"Put your hands on me and you will never hit another woman again! I ain't Nakea *or* Sonya."

"You got ten seconds to tell me or I'm going to choke ya uppity ass to death!"

"You wouldn't dare!"

"*One . . . two . . . three . . .*"

Farren could see his eyes bulging out of his eye sockets. "I dare you, *Mr. B,*" she egged him sarcastically.

"*. . . four . . . five . . . six . . . seven . . .*"

"I will send your ass to jail if you do!" She said anything to threaten his freedom and to stop him from getting violent with her. If she'd told him the truth he wouldn't believe it. She was guilty by association.

"*. . . eight . . . nine . . . ten!*"

After the tenth second Nasir draped his huge hands around her neck, and commenced to strangle the shit out of her. Farren's hands desperately smacked away at his, as she gasped for air.

AT THE COURT'S MERCY

Quinton was on his way to get some grub and was enraged to see Nasir's hands around Farren's neck.

This young boy is buggin', he thought as he yanked the Magnum's gearshift in park and ran to Farren's rescue; prying Nasir's hands off of her.

"Get the fuck off of her!"

Farren bent over, swallowing for air to get to her windpipes. Nasir was already riding high. He backed up and began swinging right hooks, sinking on Quinton's chin. After the punch landed, they grappled each other to the ground in the middle of the block.

Farren was screaming for them to stop. But she was screaming in silence; her words went unheard. Both males with enormous egos, fought like one of them were going to win a title belt in a boxing match. Soon as the police sirens sounded, their street instinct of reasoning kicked in, and they broke free. Quinton left with a busted lip and Nasir left with a scratched up back from being scraped against the concrete when they fell to the ground.

Quinton, who was once outside the love triangle, was now back in it with a point to prove—Farren was still riding his dick!

Prior to getting in his car, after the commotion died, Nasir screamed to Farren, "Where the fuck is my son?"

Farren jumped in her car and hurried off.

145

৵৽৵৽৵৽

The woman who lived in the same apartment building as Farren and Nasir: on the third floor underneath of them, heard a strange loud thump, followed by a baby, seriously wailing. She'd exchanged numbers with all her neighbors in case of emergencies. After no response from Farren's, she rushed upstairs and banged on the door with force—no result. Li'l Marv's wailing escalated.

"Something is wrong!" She reckoned, and phoned up 911.

৵৽৵৽৵৽

Nasir tailed Farren to the apartment and was greeted by their neighbor, the police and family services. The door to their apartment had been busted open, and Li'l Marv was in the custody a family service worker. An ambulance was dispatched for observation of injuries.

"Are you the parents of this child?" the family service worker asked, with a pen and notepad ready to interrogate.

Nasir replied in a somber tone, admitting the truth and manned up, "I am; she's not." He gawped at Farren, and was taken away for endangering the welfare of a child, and neglect.

It Was All a Dream

Loretta was losing her breath, and her pulse was beginning to fade away; water filled her nostrils as she began to gargle gallops of filtered chlorine water, creating large water bubbles. She was sinking, going deeper and deeper in the ten-foot end of the pool. Unable to swim, her eyes rolled to the back of her head—she was drowning—without a lifeguard to save her.

Waking up from a perfuse sweat; staring around the room as if she'd seen a ghost, Loretta aggressively held her chest. The dream was much too read; leaving her heart pounding rapidly. Marv, Sr. was in her presence again.

"Loretta, wake your ass up!" Marv was dressed in a white dashiki, tapping on the side of Loretta's head, desperately trying to get her attention. Loretta had a picture of what her love looked like, but the man she knew, her lover and friend, would never be caught wearing an outfit like this. He was a suit man.

Rubbing her eyes, she gazed at the shadow figure, bewildered. "What the fuck? Marv?"

"What the fuck, my ass! Get yo' ass up! We need to talk."

"Marv, baby," tears began to surface, making a crash landing on Loretta's nightgown. She scooted her body, holding on to Marv's waist for dear life.

"Woman, I know it's been hard since I've been gone, but you've got to get your damn life right. It's detrimental to your health." Loretta's love for Marv was so powerful it affected her will to love. But tonight, she'd be taught a lesson.

"Baby, I've missed you so much. Not a day goes by that I don't recollect the life we shared. I held that shit down and you left me!" Marv hoisted her chin to explore her love through her eyes, then slithered his supple hands underneath hers.

"That nigga had me in an undesirable situation that I tried to recover from, but that nigga carved me up!" He rose back, lifted his dashiki, allowing Loretta's hands to trace the stab wounds all over his chest, causing her to bawl with serious empathy.

"If Freeze were alive, I'd put that bitch to rest for what he's done. But his punk-ass died the same day he got out of prison."

"That's funny," Marv said. "He hasn't come through the gates. Maybe he didn't make it in." He flashed a smile at her.

"And how did you?" Loretta poked fun back at him.

"I'm one of the chosen ones."

Loretta was trying so hard to hold onto what dignity she had left, feeling hopeless on the inside. She was slowly diminishing as she remembered her emotions, the day she heard of Marv's murder.

"Come back to me, Marv!" she groused aloud.

"Loretta, I can never come back to you . . . I never left you. But since I've been gone physically, things just ain't been right with you. Girl, you're on the verge of a mental institution. They should have *been* committed yo' ass! What you need to do is stay out of those kids personal business and love them, before it's too late."

"Wait now, Marvin Bundy! It's not all my fault. If Nasir wasn't the spittin' image of you, with ho'in ways like his father, it'd be different. Sheena, she's stuck. I can't do nothing about that."

The single distinctive feature that Nasir and his father shared were the jet-black eyebrows, but the one that set them apart was bargaining. Marv Sr. wasn't a negotiator. He wouldn't argue with you. He reacted without worrying about the consequences.

"You and your half-truths and skewed-ass vision." His beef with her was fueled in measure. Her validation held no conscious. "My soul will never rest if you don't do right by these kids; they are all you have. And if *you* don't change, I'll have to haunt you forever!"

Loretta's eyeballs searched frenetically around for Marv's image, but it had disappeared. Was that another dream or was it reality? She was spooked; suffocating her mind of oxygen until she let out a scream, "Noooo!" Her measure of guilt internalized the message Marv sent to her. In that place, where she sat covered by dark cotton sheets, her heart crumbled, before she matched Marv's challenge to make it right with her children. Could the hole that she'd so dug, be patched? Or, was this the way she coped mentally, by avoiding situations to sabotage her future?

In exchange for criminal behaviors, Loretta became a destructive image of a mother haunted by love.

"I can't do this!" she bellowed from the core of her bleeding heart. *"Marv Bundy, come back to me!"*

Loretta drifted back to sleep to another dream, but this time, she woke up in a cold sweat. Holding her neck with fear, she cried, "Oh my God!" She mentally pictured death.

Guess Who's Back . . .

That morning in the holding cell, after Nasir was arrested, he was told to give contact information for Li'l Marv's mother. His primary notion was to call Nakea and tell her exactly what happened himself, but he let the police contact her to avoid being crucified. Family services simply informed him that Li'l Marv would not be released in his custody.

From the examination, they found that he had two bruised ribs, and a nasty purple and blue bruise on his arm from falling off the bed. This offense caused Nasir to lose his residential custody—custody that he slicked his way into receiving. Most likely, visitation would be taken away as well. His job would end—with a charge of endangering the welfare of a minor. Principle Hurdle had to let him go for that. Policy and procedures of the school administration warranted that . . . and the Gentlemen's program? The boys would be the ones to suffer.

Thoughts dwelled tremendously as Nasir waited to post bond. No sooner than they called Nakea, she arrived at the same precinct where Farren had turned herself in, pitching a bitch.

"Where is my son? I got a call that he's here!" Officer Salvati was on duty.

"Name please," he flatly asked her, so he could log her name in the record book.

"Nakea Perkins. My son's name is Marvin Bundy, III," she said in an angry outburst.

"Are you the mother of the child?" Officer Salvati didn't even glance at her, with his nonchalant concern. These moulies can't even try to be decent—they're useless, he mumbled.

"I just said that I was!" With her nasty tone, she was able to get his attention for a second.

"Have a seat over there." Turning his back to her, he picked up a yellow notepad and asked her loudly for others in the public seating area to hear, "Are you the custodial parent?"

"No," she reeked with unfriendliness.

"You'll need to speak with the family service worker, and sign this release of confidential information." He passed the forms through the opening as if they were contaminated trash. "They'll be out to get you shortly."

Shonda sat next to Nakea gleefully. "Girl, he don' messed up!"

Nakea's prayers had been answered. Those tearful days and shame of outsider's whispers about her losing custody of her son, those days were over. She'd hold her head high with pride now; her son was coming home. *Fuck what they heard*, she thought, *I know otherwise.*

"I wonder what happened?" Nakea asked Shonda, searching the cold, smoky corridor, where incoming individuals had to sit and wait.

"Who cares? My nephew is coming home! Don't tell me you catchin' feelings, worried about Nasir's bum-ass," she snapped at her. "Was he concerned when he took you through the ringer? Or when his bitch-ass took you for child support? See, you do dirt—you get dirt! Ha! Ha!"

"Bright and early tomorrow, I'm taking these papers to Family Court for them to drop all of that and get my custody back."

Shonda bagged up with laughter. "Now you can ask his ass, what it do? What it do, ma'fucka? What it do? Backfire on yo' ass; that's what it do!" She high-fived Nakea. "Yeah, sis, you did that! Tell dat nigga, holla back!"

While they were carrying on, acting childish about the matter, the family service worker, Ms. Bodie, advanced.

"Ms. Perkins?"

"Yes," both of them countered.

"Nakea Perkins?" Ms. Bodie reiterated.

Nakea stood up. "Right here."

"Hello." Ms. Bodie extended her hand to shake Nakea's. "I'm Ms. Bodie, the case worker assigned to this case."

Shonda was digging in her head with one hand, and the other had relaxed by her side. Both she and Nakea had jetted out the house with du-rags, tank tops, and lounge shorts on wearing Chinese slippers; rushing to find out why Li'l Marv was at the police station. Sean didn't agree to it, because he was sleep, but Shonda left her daughter with him until they came back.

"You can follow me." Ms. Bodie guided Nakea. Shonda joined them.

"I'm sorry. We need to speak to Ms. Perkins *alone*."

"Oh, no you don't. He's my nephew and I'm here in support of my sister. We are in this together!"

Ms. Bodie waited for Nakea to respond.

"She's fine." Nakea wanted Shonda with her for strength.

They passed several rooms until they reached the interrogating room. Nakea took a set at a desk where pictures taken of Li'l Marv lay, exposed. Both her and Shonda saw the brace around his chest and blew their tops.

"I will kill that bitch if she did this to my baby boy!"

"Not if I see her first!" Shonda matched the violent eruption.

Ms. Bodie asked if they could keep it under control. The other case worker's in the room scrutinized Nakea and Shonda's actions. Mrs. Bodie opened a file, and went over a series of questions with Nakea, explaining why the baby was there.

"A neighbor heard your son crying from an upstairs apartment. We assume, the father of your child's place."

Nakea confirmed with her that Li'l Marv resided with Nasir.

"When she didn't receive an answer, she contacted the authorities, who later arrived and found your son on the floor beside the bed."

Shonda covered her mouth in astonishment.

"He was taken to the hospital where they found minor injuries; two bruised ribs and other body bruises."

"Why wasn't I called?" Nakea rotated her eyes to the case workers, demanding an adequate response.

"We didn't have any contact information on you until we interviewed . . ." She scrambled to find Nasir's name in the paperwork. "Marvin Bundy, Jr., that's when you were asked to come in."

"Did you lock them both up?" Shonda ejected.

Ms. Bodie read from the paperwork, "Only the father."

"What about his girl? They live together and if he left him, she had to also! Wasn't she charged?" Nakea wanted both of them prosecuted.

"No, she wasn't, only the custodial parent."

"I don't see why not! They both left him unattended!" Shonda stated, disagreeing with Farren getting off.

"We're not exactly certain what the circumstances were; but from our conversation with Mr. Bundy, he has accepted full responsibility for the child."

"That's bullshit!" was Shonda's untamed response. She wanted Farren to get arrested too and Nakea tried her damnedest to make it happen.

"We were informed by Mr. Bundy that there's a marked history or rivalry, as he stated, between the four of you."

Nakea quickly disagreed, "We don't have no *history* other than the fact me and Nasir, Marv, Jr., have a son together!"

"Did you recently file a complaint against his girlfriend, Farren Giles?" Ms. Bodie wasn't implicating, but stating the facts from the public records.

"*That* don't have a damn thing to do with my nephew and him being left alone!" Shonda interceded.

"No, Shonda," Nakea placed her hand on her leg to still her. "Yes, I did." She played the role of the victim. "She perforated my eardrum. That's why I know she is behind this. This woman is violent and brutal!" Nakea was very suspicious. Maybe Farren did this purposely, because she was striking back for what they'd done to her.

"So, you acknowledge that this is true?"

"Yes I do, Ms. Bodie."

"Mr. Bundy also informed me that you and your . . . I take it, he's speaking about you," she said, piercing at Shonda, ". . . your sister came to Farren's job and beat her maliciously, causing her to lose her baby."

Nakea smirked, and softly let out a few grunting noises. "Mmmm . . . mmm . . . mmm! Now, I need to agree with my sister. This has absolutely nothing to do with my son!"

"But it does, we need to be assured that he is placed in a safe environment, not a hostile one. If there will be continued violence, we have to place him with someone else."

Shonda stood up and walked to the back of the room; ready to cuss Ms. Bodie out.

"There will be no violence . . . at least not in my custody. You need to direct that to his father. Now, can I sign my paperwork and get my son?"

The case workers on watch in the back of the room, signaled, and Ms. Bodie handed Nakea the clipboard to sign the release for file documentation. When the interview was completed, they were taken to rescue Li'l Marv.

They stepped into the hallway where the exit door was located, running into Nasir, who was just being released, and Farren who'd bailed him out. Nakea had a strong grit of protectiveness written all over her face, delicately holding Li'l Marv, wanting to call them both out. But she didn't want to blast them out there at the station.

"You bitch!" Shonda threatened silently to Farren, who read her lips and held back her rude response.

"You will never see my son again!" Nakea didn't take her eyes off Nasir. He made her flinch when he stepped forthright, snatching away from Farren. He didn't want to see Farren either, but was thankful she'd bailed him out.

Officer Salvati yelled through the microphone, "This is not *the hood;* it's a police station. Don't do anything stupid!" As he grabbed at his holster; not just for protection, but to intimidate and dare those in his presence.

"Nasir, ignore them and find out for yourself." Farren moved behind him making sure she didn't get hit.

Shonda came within reach. "Mind ya business, before you get fucked up again," she said as she took one more step to invade Farren's personal space, challenging her to react, so Farren would be re-arrested.

"Find out who your daughter's father is before you start defending someone else's child," Farren grilled.

The situation almost got out of hand, but Officer Salvati came from behind the glass. "If you don't stop this nonsense, I will arrest all of you for disturbing the peace. Do you understand?" he asked, ready with handcuffs in hand. The other officers behind the desk were on alert.

Shonda poked at Nasir, bringing him back to the day he insinuated she left her daughter in the house alone. "I guess you didn't heed to your own advice. Practice what you preach, nigga! C'mon, Nakea, you got the baby back, fuck them! Farren's mad 'cause she less than woman. She can't hold babies—that's all!" Those insensitive remarks hit Farren in the pit.

Nasir was facing several charges; to add to them, he had to face the judge for an outstanding warrant for assaulting another woman—Sonya! That's why he had a secured bond. Although Sonya's charges were bogus, they were filed for payback. Nasir was ordered to have no contact with Li'l Marv and Sonya. He could care less about a no-contact order with her, but, not having contact with his son, hurt him.

When Nakea rounded the corner to exit, Nasir caught a glimpse of the ONE LOVE charm, dangling from her necklace. It was then he presumed that the man who robbed Brian was Sean. The chain and the charm were destined to be in the street for sale, but did one of them have to end up on Nakea's neck? When Brian heard this, the battle on the street would begin.

He trotted out the station with Farren angrier and more disappointed than when he arrived. There were plenty of words to say to Farren; it was mostly her fault.

"Why the fuck would you leave my son in the house alone?"

"I, I—didn't mean too. He was asleep. I didn't want to wake him."

"Why'd you do that ill shit?"

Farren drove down the busy streets in morning traffic; people were on their way to work.

"How come you never answered? You was laid up with a bitch, and I was home with your son!"

"I should go on you! Don't *you ever* use my son to cover up your sneakiness! You only called to check up on me. Yo' ass left my son to get with that nigga, Quinton!" he shouted. "Take me to my mothafuckin' car! It's over between us!"

Farren had made his blood rush.

"It's over?"

"I lost my son behind you, bitch!" Nasir never spoke to her in such a way.

Farren pressed her foot on the gas pedal and floored it, holding on to the steering wheel.

"Slow this car down before we crash!" Nasir went to grab the steering wheel. Farren let up on the gas pedal, skidding tires turning the corner to her apartment. The car hadn't come to a complete stop, but Nasir didn't care, he rushed out to get his belongings and go!

When we forgive evil we do not excuse it, we do not tolerate it, we do not smoother it. We look the evil full in the face, call it what it is, let its horror shock and stun and enrage us, and only then do we forgive it.
Lewis B. Smedes

Same As It Ever Was

Eric, Sheena's man and her son's father, had pressed her to resolve her issues with her mother, for the sake of their son. It was important to him that his son became acquainted with her grandmother; for his own mother and grandmother passed away a year apart. Family was embedded in him. He felt it necessary for his son to be united with both sides of his family.

"Call her, Sheena . . . what's it gonna hurt?"

"Eric, you don't know my mother. She doesn't care about how I feel."

"People change, Sheena."

"Not her—I'm telling you it's a waste of time. I'm tired of being hurt by her. Every time I reach out to her, she throws stones at me, setting me back further. *You,* of all people, *know this!*"

"But the therapist made it clear that it's best to air out all of your feelings to her."

Sheena signified. "I've done that! What more can I say?"

"Find it in your heart to do it for our son, Sheena."

The plea in Eric's shaking voice put pressure on Sheena to surrender, or attempt to deliver a truce with

163

Loretta. She would do this, but only to show Eric how plastic her mother was to her.

"I'll do it, but you'll have to come with me."

"I'm right by your side, baby; let's do it!"

⋇⋇⋇⋇⋇

Loretta was parlaying in her front room, watching the neighborhood kids on her block run back and forth through the fire hydrant that had water pouring out from it. August was three weeks away from ending, and school was soon to begin. The kids were enjoying their last bit of summer fun. Summer always stirred-up the worst in black folk, especially when the heat was too much to bear.

"Fran, look at these crazy kids. As children, we used to do that. We'd have one of the old men on the block bust open a fire hydrant, and play in the water for hours, until the city shut it down."

"Those kids are having a grand old time—just being kids."

"You know I miss those days."

Francine frowned. "What? Playing with a fire hydrant?"

"No, silly—living free."

"Shit! You damn near live free now. How much you pay, ten, twenty dollars in rent? You lucky!"

AT THE COURT'S MERCY

"Fuck you! I'm not talking about housing. I'm talking about when my mind was free. I still haven't fully come around since Marv died, you know."

"We all know you throwed off." Francine gestured making circles with her finger by her temple. "With ya nutty bee-hind!" She tried to make a joke out of it.

"I'm serious, Fran, my mind is still fucked up."

Women are adept at carrying on conversations with their eyes; and when Francine looked into Loretta's, she knew her friend was really battling with her sanity. It was past the understanding of how to deal with her loss, because she'd lost one of the most important factors—how to love and to let go, when it adversely affects your health.

"Loretta, things will never be same. Baby, Marv is gone. You gotta close that chapter of your life and move on. If you keep reflecting on the past, you will miss things that are currently going on. Think about it. How do you think the kids handle this? They've weathered the storm with you, and you keep shutting the door on them when they need you."

"It's not about them anymore, Fran, they are grown! What about me?"

Francine faced Loretta. "It's not too late to play catch up, gurl . . . when you've messed up. They may be of age, but they deserve to feel a mother's love!"

"I've been having dreams of Marv lately," Loretta blurted out.

Francine threw her hands in the air. Loretta wasn't hearing her at all. "Damn you, Loretta! "He's haunting me." Her eyes pleaded for Fran to understand.

"His ass need to! Maybe he's the only one who can bring you back to current day."

"Guess what that fool keeps saying?"

"What?" Francine temporary halted.

"The same thing you are."

"And I hope you're gonna take heed!"

"That man still love him, some me!" Loretta spread her arms open wide, and began clapping her hands together like a joyous toddler.

It was no use and Francine knew it. While Loretta came back around physically, she would never be there one hundred percent, mentally.

"I'm gone, Loretta. I think someone's knocking at your door."

"See who it is for me. I don't feel like having company."

Francine opened the door and warmly greeted Sheena, Eric, and the baby.

"Gimme my smooches, baby. Wish I could stay, but I've got some catching up to do. Your mother is in the there. Eric, don't start nothin' it and it won't be nothin' . . . flexing all those muscles."

"*Aunt Fran.*" Sheena chuckled; but her chuckle dissipated when they didn't receive a warm welcome from Loretta.

"What y'all doing here?" Loretta sneered.

Sheena rolled her eyes at Eric, who nudged her to sit down.

"How you doing, Ms. Loretta." Eric went over and kissed her on the cheek. Immediately, she smeared the kiss away.

"Get off of me!" She wasn't used to showing open affection; even if it was innocent. Sheena and Nasir could count on each hand the number of times Loretta gave them hugs, and said I love you.

"We don't have to do this, Eric." Sheena tried effortlessly to get him to back out of this.

"It's cool, baby. Yes we do."

"If you say so."

They went back and forth as if Loretta weren't standing there. Sheena had confronted her before, but this time was different—they were face to face. Eric provided Sheena with continual emotional support. If it hadn't been for him, Mom Flossy, and Nasir, she didn't know what would have become of her.

The conversation started off a little rocky, but Sheena didn't let that deter her.

"Hi Loretta." Eric gave Sheena that disrespectful look. "Mom." She switched up. "I came to make peace with you."

"Peace? My life been in shambles for years; there's no such thing as peace." Loretta mused at her daughter's way of thinking.

"You think? Anyway, Grandmom's been asking for you. She said you haven't been to see her in a while."

"Why is it that I always have to cater to her got damn needs?"

Sheena cringed in her seat. She and Nasir didn't play when it came down to speaking against the woman that raised them.

"My grandmother took care of us when you couldn't! You have some nerve! She can barely stand up from her wheelchair." Sheena came to Grandmom Flossy's defense without thinking twice.

"Mommie just wants attention." Still pouting, Loretta said, "She's been like that for years."

In that instance Sheena went against Eric's request to make this work between her and her mother.

"Grandmom suffered a stroke, barely making it. By the grace of God, she made it through like the trooper she is! And not one day did she forget to make sure her grandkids were okay. So, don't you talk like that about her *only* wanting attention!"

"I'm sorry that you feel that way, Sheena," Loretta responded casually, toying with her indisputable emotions. "But if you don't like it, stay away like you've been!

Disturbing as it was, Eric rubbed Sheena's back in relief, showing comfort and support.

"I told you she doesn't care about nobody. It used to be she only cared about Nasir, but now, it's all about Loretta." She fidgeted. "Not once has she asked to see her grandson."

"Why get attached to a child I rarely get a chance to see? I don't have to ask Nakea to see Li'l Marv. Why should I have to ask you? You either bring him or you don't—simple as that!"

"Fuck this, Eric!" Sheena cursed loudly.

Loretta politely got up from her seat and collared Sheena up against the wall. "When you're ready to test me, I want you to try it! Otherwise, don't you ever come in my house disrespecting me like that! You, your man and *your* baby, can get the hell outta here!"

Eric's mouth dropped. Sheena yanked free from her and darted to the door.

"Don't even worry, baby. Loretta's grown to be who she's gonna die as—an unloving miserable woman!" With that, Eric cradled his son in one arm and embraced his woman with his other, and they left in the same pleasant manor as they came.

For Sheena, the road of life had many ups and downs and turns and twists, but her sacrifice to stay strong through her tribulations was a gift from God. When thy mother and father forsake thee, the Lord will take you in.

Go 'head and Cry

"The protection order states you're supposed to be one thousand feet away from him," Loretta contended with Nasir, while she babysat Li'l Marv for Nakea.

"But I'm your son! How can you deny me of seeing my own son? Forget that court order!" Nasir respectively argued.

It was undecipherable how Loretta, his on mother, adhered to the court order. This devastated him and he now inherited Sheena's pain.

"At least bring him to the window so I can see him," he urged of her, talking through the glass window. Loretta had changed the locks and he no longer had access to get in.

"I can't do that. Thank your woman for the position she put you in! Nakea told you Farren wasn't to be trusted."

"To hell with what she thinks! If I asked her today to get back with me, she'd drop Sean and let me see my son!"

"You have a pending court case. Don't ruin your chances of ever seeing your son again. Don't violate the rules. I'm doing this for your own good. If your father were—"

"Don't put him in this. My father would never take sides with an outsider. Family meant the world to him. Leave him out of this!"

"That's what you think! If that were true, you'd know about Lena's son," she blabbed out. "Leave! Nakea is getting purchase of care from the State so the baby can continue going to Lois Kiddie 1, 2, 3. Go torment Mrs. Lois; maybe she'll let you see him."

Thought bubbles popped in Nasir's head. Lena's son—what did that equate to? How was her son associated? Though he had breathing space, the stress in his chest came down a notch.

Mrs. Lois, a sweet, motherly woman, knew the importance of a father. To deny him of seeing his son wasn't in her spirit. Court order in place or not, she'd witnessed, and could vouch that Nasir was a good father.

Loretta was right; with a pending court case, he needed to be extra cautious with his moves. Making the wrong adjustment could cost him jail time. Furthermore, he had some serious explaining to do with Principal Hurdle, before the information leaked out. It was good for Nasir that school was out and the summer program was only operating. However, there were less than three and half weeks before the new school year started. A major headline exposing this kind of information by a staff member, would affect the credibility of Charter Elementary.

Before Nasir traveled that way, he had to talk with Mom Flossy. She was home with her visiting nurse, watching the Maury Povich show. Both the nurse and Mom Flossy were laughing at the ridiculous use of body language the females were using, when it came down to convincing the crowd that their child had features like the alleged father who requested the paternity test.

Nasir came in with his head lowered. "Hey, Grandmom, can we talk?" He excused the visiting nurse for the remainder of her time.

"Talk to me, baby." She patted the empty seat next to her for him to sit down. Nasir was on the verge of breaking down. The world surrounding him crumbled in less than five days. His mind fought evil thoughts that he wanted to act upon.

But real men didn't cry—they stomached their problems. They didn't cry a river like soft men do as the myth is told. However, this myth was negated as it related to him. He chose to cry a river to cleanse his soul. This was a crisis point in his life; nothing to prove, *but* the truth that he was human.

Mom Flossy's grandmother's intuition was in full gear. "Its okay, grandson." She opened her arms to him.

He rested his head on her shoulder fighting back the tears. "It's kinda hard out here for a pimp." He tried to make light of his problems, but couldn't hold back any longer, and the tears reigned.

Mom Flossy rubbed his arm in circular motions and told him, "Crying is like taking your soul to the laundry mat—go on and cry, baby."

If Lyfe Jennings only knew what impact he made when he wrote that song. Nasir cried and shared his dilemma with his grandmom.

Never let your head hang down. Never give up and sit and grieve. Find another way. And don't pray when it rains if you don't pray when the sun shines.

Satchel Paige

You Want the Truth?

Stationed in front of the school, Nasir settled, contemplating how he was going to explain to his boss that he was arrested for neglect, and endangering the welfare of a child—his child. How could he argue his point? Would the district care if he hadn't been found guilty yet? The charges were on his record. Still, he was guilty until proven innocent.

With an unreadable face, Nasir requested a meeting with Principal Hurdle through his secretary. Reluctant to involve him, he knew that it had to be done. A man had to do what a man had to do—face the consequences of his actions.

Busy reviewing reports, Principal Hurdle hinted for Nasir to come in. The stress of a black man running a predominantly minority-filled school was trying. Enrollment was down, but if parents were knowledgeable of the information Nasir was there to reveal, more were sure to withdraw their children. It was impressive that the Gentlemen's program bred and increased positive male behaviors, but would this override his charges? Credit was given to Nasir and Counselor Brad for committing themselves to helping the group of young, underprivileged men grow into responsible, active citizens in their communities. However, Nasir's actions reflected his character. How would parents respond to the allegations made against him?

"How's it going, Mr. B?" Principal Hurdle removed the report covering his face to give Nasir his undivided attention.

"It's hard to call." Nasir tried to remain positive without seeming nervous.

"Well, you will be happy to know that the State has accepted and approved the grant for the upcoming school year, for additional activities and trips for the Gentlemen's program," he spread the news with discernible earnestness.

Suddenly realizing the importance of his presence in the boy's lives killed his will to share the ill-timed news. "That's good, I'm glad they approved it."

"Make sure your plans are solid. We can take this program and model it statewide!"

Nasir fiddled with his fingers. "I have some good news and I have some not so good news; which do you want to hear first?" he asked his superior whose merriment washed-out to a face perturbed.

"Not so good news first." He selected.

"Yesterday I was arrested and charged with neglect, endangering the welfare of a child . . . and third degree assault."

Principal Hurdle balled up his fist securely and hit his desk three times. *"Jesus!"* He slanted back in his leather executive chair. "And what good news can come to coat that news?"

"The good news is I haven't been convicted." Nasir hoped with this bit of news, he would bear with him until the cases were heard in court.

"My Lord! If the press gets a hold of this information, they will have my job in the classified section of the paper the next day!"

Nasir deformed his mouth to the side.

"What have you gotten yourself into, son?"

Nasir didn't leave out one detail as he poured out his story, and when he was finished telling it, he asked the question he was longing to get answered, "With the charges pending, does this mean you have to fire me?"

That was a tough query for Principal Hurdle. State regulations prohibited criminal offenses that included any involvement with or against minors. "We can play this out until you are officially convicted, but I do need to forewarn you, if you are convicted—taking a plea even—termination is inevitable. Also . . ." he said in dismay, ". . . If parents or the press find out, I'll have to let you go immediately. There's nothing else I can do about it." He released the secured fists he made with his hands and placed them together as if in prayer, and placed them on his lips.

"I understand." All the work that he'd put in was blackened with one incident.

"Son, if you plan on making a change in your life, you have to do it full circle, not halfway. Bad always outweighs the good, no matter how much good you do. Deal with the problems you contributed to this mayhem. You've inflamed an injustice not to yourself, but all the people that stood behind you. Most importantly: those of us that gave you a second chance," he ungainly stressed. "Your personal life is your personal life, but when it starts affecting the kids, I have a major concern for the protection of my students."

Nasir focused keenly on a man with vast experience in educating individuals. "I appreciate everything you and your wife have done for me, believe me. If it's not too much," he bartered, "please don't talk this over with Mrs. Hurdle; she'd be really displeased with me."

"True, indeed! I'll keep my mouth shut and let's pray that others do the same."

Nasir returned to his hideout crib and assembled with Brian, bagging up twenties of cocaine. He'd put Brian up on his situation as well. Nasir took a seat on the sectional sofa opposite of him.

"We need to have a serious conversation, man."

Brian had a razor chopping off chunks of cooked cocaine depositing the hard brick rocks into small baggies.

"What up?" he asked, working diligently to bag up two hundred, twenties. "Help me bag up this shit while you talk."

Nasir took a new razor from the box and cut away; breaking off fat twenties: pieces the size of Chicklets gum. "I know who hit you up."

Brian stopped, raised his eyes to level Nasir's, "Word! Who?"

"It was Sean; Nakea's man."

Brian sat up straight. "Are you sure?"

"Man, that bitch Nakea is wearing your 'One Love' charm on her neck. She don't have the necklace, but it's damn sure your charm."

"She could've got that shit off the street hot. You know how niggas do when they swipe shit!"

"Think about it . . . that nigga got it bad for me, and they know you the only dude eatin' lovely from the block. Chauncey been slippin' comments to our supplier. He still don't know I fuck wit' his connect. So, yo, my man keep telling me Chauncey hatin' on us; *specially you* 'cause he think I bowed out." He had Brian thinking. "Any other nigga would have dumped two in you and ran up in your spot! Why would they rob you for a few ounces, a few dollars, and some jewels, and not get in your crib where the safe is? It was done to shake you up, put you on alert, man—pay attention!"

"Right, it don't add up."

"That's what I'm sayin'. Chauncey rolls like that—he ain't no killa. He wants to find out the source behind you!"

"But how you think Sean got involved?"

"Dude broke and hungry; a dreadful combination. He couldn't come to you for work, so who's the next best source on the block?"

"Chauncey," they tied in unison.

"He's the link," Brian concluded.

"Lemme play this out. I've got a lot of people to confront. Farren, Nakea, Sonya, Lena . . . these women gotta mafucka goin' crazy!"

"I heard that, man."

"I think I know a way to get at Chauncey. And Sonya don't know it yet, but she's gonna help."

"Whatever! I'm wit' it," Brian wanted to get whoever was implicated with his robbery.

"Don't shoot the gun prematurely when you see either of these niggas; continue on like its all good."

"I got you, playa. Make sure you take your own advice into consideration. You can get a hothead like this," Brian snapped his fingers. "Yo, so are you really moving out of Farren's?"

"Without looking back! Man, I lost custody of my son because she was chasing after the next man. I can't forgive her for that!"

Brian played the devil's advocate. "But you can't put that all on her. You sent li'l man over there and got wit' another honey for the night. And on some real shit, she just lost *your* baby and you sent *your* son by *another woman*, over there at a time like that. Think about it."

"Granted," Nasir bucked, "she lost a baby, but I loss one too . . . a son that I had custody of. Now, nigga, it's a done deal!"

"It's closed for discussion then." Brian shut up.

"My visit is scheduled to see my Uncle Stan on Saturday," Nasir concluded their conversation on another note.

The ultimate measure of a man is not where he stands in moments of comfort and convenience, but where he stands at times of challenge and controversy.
Dr. Martin Luther King, Jr.

Cell Block H

Stan aged over the years; once stubbly black hair covered his head—now, it was satiated with gray. The broad frame Stan had slimmed, but his sleekness complemented the studious glasses he wore, reflecting a man with knowledge. Nasir couldn't remember when they last encountered. Years and years ago, in his pre-teens, Francine carried him along on visits.

Stan was housed in minimum security of the H wing, where low risk inmates stayed. Over the years, he'd become a model prisoner, posing no threats to staff or fellow inmates. The last month, Stan had been listening to all the young inmates toss the names, B-Right, Chauncey and Nasir around; affiliating them with the drug game. He was adamant about Francine relaying the message to Nasir for him to visit. Nasir wasn't going to end up like his father—in the grave at a young age.

Passing through security, butterflies ballooned in Nasir's stomach.

This ain't the place for me, he thought.

The visiting room was small, and unlike many prisons where inmates sat across from you, partitioned by three-inch thick glass, visitors were only separated at this prison by a table. Stan acclaimed Nasir right away, and hugged him like he'd never have a chance to hug him again.

"Nephew!" he greeted him. "In your father's image! Marv spit you out. Loretta didn't have nothin' to do with that."

Nasir smiled. "Hey, Uncle Stan." No matter how independent Nasir had become, Stan was actually his Godfather, acting like an uncle since he was Big Marv's best friend. And Nasir humbly respected him as such.

"How have you been?"

"Right now," Nasir spoke truthfully, "I'm in a bad way."

"How so?" Stan asked, but knew to some extent what was going on in the streets.

"I'm on the verge of losing my job. I lost custody of my son behind my girl and . . ."

"And," Stan butted in, ". . . the game don't change—only the players. Let's talk about that!"

Quietly, Nasir sat taunting himself, feeling suspended by life. "I didn't get out. It was too much money to be made. Me and my boy, Brian, partnered up and did that! We came up in the game."

"There are consequences that come with the game. It's too risky," Stan alerted him.

"I know, I'm feeling the repercussions of some of them. It's like somebody took an eraser to a part of my life and erased parts away. There's a void—something's missing."

Stan pulled dead bones, lying under the surface, out. "There will always be a void. But what part of the game is knocking off your dad's old joint?"

Nasir felt low and went on to explain, "Uncle Stan, I didn't know at first. Lena came onto me when I was sixteen years old. In the park with my boys, I gained major points for scoring with her. It was all in building my rep. Then one day, she starts breaking down, telling me she was in love with my father. Of course, I'm stumped, and thought she was pulling my coat. But when she retrieves a photo album and I see my dad . . . *and you*," he added, "posted up all over the place. I'm like, damn! No pun intended, but I felt real fucked up!"

"Did you leave her alone when you found out this information?"

Nasir nodded no. "I'm guilty of that. The damage was done, so I continued boning her. Man, Lena's a freak like that! I'ma young boy spraying hot piss on her. Man, her freak-ass love golden showers. I'm bustin' off in her mouth, gettin' anal and dig . . . she even likes to be defecated on!"

Stan was so disgusted, not at Nasir, but how Lena took advantage of him knowing her history with Marv Sr.

"Are you still dealing with her?"

"Not like that."

"Don't fuck with her no more." Stan was stern. "She's an evil, wicked, ruthless, bitch!"

Nasir acknowledged and accepted his demand.

"Lena's a whore from way back. I don' fucked her, and plenty of other niggas have. She'll fuck your son when he gets of age, to get back at you!"

Apologetically, Nasir hinted for forgiveness.

"Lena tricked for your father. A lot of women sold pussy for him. And many of them fell in love with their pimp. That was his job, and he was clever and sufficient with his delivery. He got up in their heads, psyching them up to sell their ass. He was a true *pimp*, not the unadulterated watered- down, third generation pimp. He was from the first string!

Against the rules, Lena got pregnant. Your mom was his main woman." He saw Nasir's questionable look. No son wanted to find out his mother was a prostitute. "No, Loretta wasn't selling pussy—only dope. Telling Loretta that Lena was pregnant, that was murder-suicide. So he kept it on the low. Plus, he didn't know whose baby it was, but as her pimp, it was his responsibility to tend to her."

Nasir inhaled. The thought of Lena's son being his brother concerned him. *That's what my mom meant when she spat that out at me!* He was mesmerized.

"Since Lena disobeyed orders, your dad kept her on the block until she was nine months pregnant. Lena despised your mother, blaming her. Then, when Lena found out Loretta was pregnant with you, she showed out."

"Was the child his?" Nasir warily hoped not.

"It wasn't proven until the day before your father was murdered." He tripped over his tongue.

Nasir's upper body lumbered over. The guard on watch told him to pick his head up. "Of all the men you say she's been with, my dad was the father?"

"It wasn't ordered by the courts. Your dad took the boy to a private doctor and had blood drawn to determine if he was his. The test proved it, but who in the hell was gon' tell Loretta, when she'd just sentenced to an 18-year bid?"

"But you were in jail, how are you so sure?"

"Francine was the one that went with him."

Suppressed feelings were brought to surface by his body language. Nasir was troubled all over.

"I realize it hurts, nephew, but Francine didn't want to further complicate things back then. How were we to know that as a teen, you would have relations with this woman? We did it to protect your mother!"

"But, Uncle Stan, I've been boning my only brother's mother. Not just that—I've never had a chance to build a relationship with him!"

Stan played it calm. "The points and rep with your boys, don't add up now, do they?"

"Hell no! What's my brother's name?'

"Quinton."

Imaginary tons of bricks fell upon Nasir's shoulders. "What's his last name?" It was mandatory that it be out in the open.

"Uh, Quinton Shelby, Lena's maiden name. Your father, forbid Lena to give him the Bundy name."

Nasir had never physically come in contact with Lena's son that he knew of; however, there was one Quinton that he knew of—Farren's ex-boyfriend. It couldn't be him!

For the remainder of the visit, Nasir listened to Stan preaching to him about leaving the game, but he wasn't listening. He wanted the visit over with, so he could address Lena immediately. But Stan's last words touched him, "The game brings destruction. It's like eating fish and spittin' out the bones. You know it's some danger in it, but you still take the risk. Don't get choked off a bone, godson!"

*Sometimes when I'm alone, I cry
because I am on my own.*
Tupac Shakur

Through the Motions

Nasir called Lena a hundred times, and her voicemail answered each time. Dying to know Quinton's last name, Nasir called Farren, but her response was the same. Going through this made Nasir crave to see his son, but he was forbidden to make contact with him.

The first time he stopped by Mrs. Lois', he was a little doubtful, even though they had a long conversation about his situation. Mrs. Lois wasn't trying to lose twenty-five years of service and dedication behind him, and she adamantly voiced that to him. The arrangement was one hour per week, supervised in her home, but only during naptime. Nasir was there faithfully, trying to spend what little time he could with his son. Visits made him more vengeful than before. It was demoralizing to sneak around like a wanted convict, just to see his son, when he'd done no wrong.

It was mid-afternoon and Nasir hurried up to the courthouse steps, after just leaving Mrs. Lois'. Today, a judge would address the assault charge Sonya filed against him. He checked his name in with the court clerk, and asked if Sonya had registered as well—she hadn't. That led to a sigh of relief. If she failed to show, the court appointed attorney—the public defender— informed him that the case would be dropped. Thoughts chased each other through his mind. Should he have hired a real attorney? Was it a risk to settle for a public defender? If Sonya were to show, he'd need a good lawyer to stand in his defense.

Sonya pranced in confidently, spotted Nasir, and made her way to the hard, brown bench he was seated on.

"Hey, cutie." The very thought of having one cased dropped made him humble; not rude, as he could be to her.

"Sonya, what's this bullshit about?" The fluster in his voice was discerned.

"I won't go through with this if you agree to one thing," she purred with seducing eyes. He knew what that *one thing* would be. The question was, would she really drop the charges?

"Agree to what?"

"Agree to get some of this good pussy, that's all I'm asking." Her intent was revealed—she wanted to seduce him. The thought came, and went—went, and came. If sleeping with her would alleviate one case, then his chances of keeping his job were good. He'd agree. This wasn't about anybody else—this was his fate.

"A'ight, when?" As annoyed as he was with Sonya, he was accepting to her unexpected request.

"Tonight. Not at my mom's either. I want a hotel suite. We're gonna pull an all-nighter!"

Skeptic, he asked, "How do I know for sure you're going to drop the charges?"

"By me leaving, that's how." Sonya pinned this on him. "This is between you and I; not Chauncey and ya chick. Neither one of them have to know."

"Sure. I believe you," he responded dryly. "Just getta steppin'." Leaving, she brushed her huge breasts pass his face.

Nasir held his palms to his forehead. *What have I gotten myself into? Should I go through this?*

Court of Common Pleas was much different than Family Court. He'd soon have to face the judges in Family Court for charges against his son—his own flesh and blood. The public defender pulled Nasir to the side. "I'd advise you to take a plea when they offer it on your next court date."

"I'm not accepting no plea!" he strictly stated. "What happened to, 'if she doesn't show'?"

"That still stands, but I believed she checked in. If it was an error, you'll be good, but if it wasn't, take my advice and think about the plea. You won't last in trial when they get a hold of these photos." He slid a Kodak envelope full of pictures. Nasir opened the

193

photographs, astonished by the black eyes, busted lip and swollen blood vessels on Sonya's face. Puzzled, he asked, "What are these for?"

"Those are the pictures of the victim!"

Nasir contemplated whether he should go through the motion or, take his chance. Sonya was a fucking nut case!

The judge called for Nasir and Sonya, but only Nasir stood. He called for Sonya a second and third time, before deciding to dismiss the charges. It was now time for Nasir to take care of his side of the bargain.

Grateful that he got off, it was now delivery time. Comfort Suites had the cheapest suites rates for the night. Letting Brian in on this, he had Bones, a faithful customer, register the room in her name.

"Are you sure you wanna do thi, dawg?" Brian said, uneasily. "What if Farren or Chauncey find out? Big mouth Sonya gon' tell it," he guaranteed.

"Fuck both of them and I mean that! This shit is about me. My charges were dropped—she came through—I owe her."

"Listen to this! All the shit she put you through? Nigga, she owes you! You don't owe that ho shit!" Brian was extremely entitled to feel that way.

"Man, you're right, but now I'm back in. Just make sure you keep your cellie on tonight."

AT THE COURT'S MERCY

"A'ight boss. You call the shots. Don't let that stupid girl come between you and Farren. I understand you're mad, but Farren's a keeper. And, if you slip up with her, a brotha might take off where you left off. I ain't scared to eat leftovers playa," he tantalized.

"It's over for us. You can eat it if you want!" Nasir had a rigid expression, but wondered if Brian meant what he said.

Never would Nasir risk picking Sonya up, so he told her to catch a cab to the room.

"Sonya, meet me at Comfort Suites on King Street at seven p.m."

"Damn, we startin' off early. Dat's what's up!"

Swiftly he responded, "That's more time for us. You want that right?"

"I know that's right! I knew a nigga missed this ass. When you coming to get me?"

"Just told you I'm not; catch a cab."

Like a chicken-head she asked, "You gon' pay for it?"

"Of course, girl, now hurry and get yo' ass over here."

Before getting the room, he readied himself with a gallon of Remy Red, Sonya's favorite. Ordering the smut channel on pay per view helped to get him aroused. The telephone in the room sounded, disrupting his illusion of the big Latin, plump, satin booty that rode another man with her ass high in the air moaning, *Oooh, Papi!*

"Okay, I'm coming down," he said to the clerk, then headed downstairs to pay for Sonya's cab.

Sonya was downstairs in the lobby of the hotel with a mustered colored tube dress on that could pass as a shirt—a small, tight shirt. Nasir paid the cab driver and escorted Sonya upstairs on the elevator. She could have said anything as long as she didn't start talking crazy. If she did, he would end the night early.

"A bitch came through for you, didn't she?"

With the charges dropped and being out of the courtroom, Nasir wasn't as kind. "If you'd never gone up there with that bogus shit, I would've never been trying to defend myself. Then, to hand them those pictures like I fucked you up—I should fuck you up right now for that!"

"Unh, unh, unh, I will take it there . . . with more photos if you do." She laughed it off.

"Yo, you are seriously missing some marbles, girl."

"Only for you. How come you don't fuck wit' me no mo'? Why you cut me off like that?"

"That's the past. You got a man, you don't need me." He reeled her in.

"Fuck Chauncey! Dat nigga ain't shit! You know he hates your guts, right? He feels like you pissed on him, came up in the game off his name."

"This ain't no set up, is it? 'Cause yo, I'll call up some niggas to dump ya ass!"

"You ain't gon' kill nothin' or let nothin' die! Fake-ass wangsta," she said as the elevator bell rang to the eighth floor, in route to room eight hundred seventeen.

"Keep talking that fly shit." He mashed her head. Sonya's hands felt his chiseled chest in a way to entice him. "Save that until we get in the room."

He used the security key to open the door, then dropped it down on the mahogany dresser, near the lamp. Slowly, he filled each glass—his without ice; this called for a straight shot.

Sonya lifted her glass. "Let's toast to us." With her glass raised, Nasir left her hanging.

"Drink that shit and quit trippin'! This is a one time thing."

"That's what you think," Sonya whispered. She sat down in the chair next to the bed. "You know Chauncey fuck wit' dat young boy Sean," she was loose at the mouth, not loyal to anyone.

"Yeah?"

"Yeah, and guess what? Dat nigga is fuckin' an old moms that drive a blue tricked out Mag!"

Nasir went to get another drink. That blue Mag she was talking about, had to be the one he'd seen Quinton driving. Putting two and two together, he came up with four—Quinton was Lena's boy. That night, Quinton didn't accompany Farren; she was meeting him at his house. It was confirmed and this blew him away. *Fuck!* He wanted to holler, but took a tired approach.

"Yeah?" He played it cool once more, but felt like running out the room straight to Lena's crib.

That manipulating, lying bitch! He thought. *She used me to get back at my mom. And what's fucked up is, she knew my girl was her son's old flame! That grimy bitch!* He was hostile. *That's why she won't answer my calls. I was nothing more than a pawn to her.*

"Cut the shit, Sonya, what the fuck you really want? You trying to set me the fuck up?" Getting leery he jumped in her face.

"No." She smacked her lips. "All I want to do is fuck; to let dem bitches know, Sonya can still get it!" she said, coming out of her tube-top dress, exposing her big Black, hardened nipples and mustered thong that had EAT ME on her pussy paw, which matched her dress. The string in the back of her thong sank in around her nice-sized buttered ass. Despite his efforts, Nasir instantly hardened.

"Damn, girl!" He watched Sonya touch spots that he loved touching on a woman.

"You know I bring the raucous, baby! Dat's what Sonya's about." Her words came out just the way they were meant. When she was around, there was always raucous. She bent over in front of Nasir, allowing him to smack her ass. And like jam, it shook, but went right back into place. The temptation was overwhelming. If she was going to kiss and tell, Nasir didn't care; not at this moment.

Fuck that! Nasir thought.

Sonya had his rock-hard penis out of his pants that were halfway down. Using her hands to ruffle them all the way down, she leaned in closer and did a few tricks with her jaws; juggling Nasir's balls in them.

"You sho' is a pro!" he moaned.

When she finished giving him a head job, she, without delay, inched her ass onto his manhood, as he was cumming. Nasir was caught up in the moment, but he wasn't that stupid.

"Not without a rubber," he stressed to her, but she'd already dropped down on his dick, receiving the last bit of cum that squirted out. Robustly, he yanked himself away.

"Put that dick back in my bubblin' pussy! It's calling your name!" With her whorish ways, she spread her legs open and her pussy lips smiled at him. "Nigga,

I've been waiting for this day since the last time I fucked you!"

"Did you bring any condoms?" Immovable, he asked.

"No, boy, I didn't need one to suck ya dick!" The way Sonya got down was *raw!* "No I didn't, but I'm safe."

"Not safe enough for me." Nasir hoisted his pants up and fastened his belt. "I'll be right back. I'm going to get some rubbers." He conned her.

Gathering what he came with, he said to himself, "Thanks for that blazin'-ass head!" Purposely, he left the whore $50 on the bathroom sink when he went to use it before leaving.

Sonya waited and waited for him to return, drinking the last of the Remy Red. After three hours passed, she realized Nasir played her again.

"I'm gonna get you, Nasir, and this time, you'll pay heavily! she cried.

You have to look at reality . . . once you cloud your vision with sentimentally . . . you are in trouble.

Coleman Young

What's Pleasing to One, May Not Be Pleasing to Another.

"Sean! Guess what, baby?" Nakea drew the covers back from his face as he lay on their new queen, steel-framed canopy bed. As a child, Nakea dreamed of having one. Sean made that dream a reality when he surprised her with its delivery. New pillows, sheets, and comforter set, covered the bed. Shonda felt a tinge of jealousy since her and her daughter still slept on a mattress.

"What?" woozily, he replied.

"I got my son back!" She wanted him to be as joyous as she was; however; Sean had not too long ago come home from being out, grinding all night. Now, he was catching up on his rest.

"Good! Now that bitch-ass nigga don't have no reason to come 'round. The next time he calls, tell him, make it his last time!" He threw the covers back over his face. "Since you got me up, go fix me some breakfast."

AT THE COURT'S MERCY

Nakea exited the room, watching Shonda stand with the front door open. "Bones get high all day long. That son of hers be filthy; wearing the same clothes for two and three days."

"Wash them for him instead of talking about him. He's only a little boy; he don't know!"

"Did you see that pile of clothes I have of my own to wash?"

"Adding a few outfits won't cause no damage to the load."

Shonda pushed her body further out the door. "Good! There's the mailman." She ran to get her Chinese slippers.

"You act like its check day."

"Nakea don't get cute, okay? I'm waiting for some mail."

"Ain't shit coming but bills, and you don't pay not nay one of 'em."

Shonda flipped her middle finger in gesture, and went to meet the mailman. Nakea opened the fridge to retrieve the pork sausage, eggs and cheese. Nasir didn't eat pork, but Sean did. He'd studied to be a Muslim momentarily, while in jail, but cancelled that when he found he couldn't eat pork.

She smiled at her son, swinging in his Playmate swing. The social worker approved her childcare, which was a major relief to her pocket. She couldn't afford to pay $125 weekly, for childcare. With subsidized daycare, she only paid one dollar and forty-two cents per day; seven dollars and ten cents per week. That fee was more than affordable; it was damn near getting care for free.

Shonda flew through the door waving an envelope in Nakea's face.

"Aaaah, bitch, I told you my Section 8 was coming through!"

"Lemme see." Nakea opened the sausage, and put the portions in an aluminum pan to place in the oven.

"Wash you hands first." Shonda had a cheesy grin on her face. Nakea ran water over her hands and blotted them dry with a hand towel. She reached for the envelope and unfolded the paper inside. It was from the Section 8 office. Shonda was scheduled to receive her voucher for housing. All she needed to do was bring her current income documentation. Nakea was happy for her, but frustrated that she wasn't the one with a voucher. Her housing was project-based, which meant, she couldn't transfer anywhere. Shonda, on the other hand, could use her voucher to transfer to any state that had a voucher program.

"I'm outta here! I can't wait for my appointment. I'm asking them to immediately transfer my shit."

"Why would you move to a place you know nothing about?"

"Same reason why you moved here. Don't hate! You can bounce out wit' me. You know how we do!"

"I can't leave." Nakea lurched down.

"Why not?"

Sean slowly made his way to the kitchen with a pair of boxers on without a shirt, showing his chest hair. "She ain't leavin' me—that's why!" he answered for her.

"I don't know why not. All you do is beat her ass."

"Shonda!" Nakea cut in. "Don't start, okay? Not today!"

"I bet he betta not trip when the kids in da house. That big machete in that corner . . ." Sean and Nakea looked over. ". . . That's what you use to protect yourself when I ain't here! I purchased it just for that reason."

"Keep talkin' and I'ma use it on you!"

"Jump, nigga!" Shonda snatched up the machete. "That would be the last got damn time you hit someone. I'll dig all in here." She pointed to his chest cavity.

"Nakea, put two slices of bread in the toaster and hurry up with my sandwich. A nigga hungry!"

"A nigga need to brush his teeth, wash his ass, and put some clothes on. Dat's what a nigga need to do." Shonda curled up her lips.

All the mouth Nakea had died down when Sean was present. His last episode with the gun, made her respect his gangsta.

AT THE COURT'S MERCY

If life is a game, these are the rules.

Cherie Carter-Scott, Ph.D

Reminisce on the Times We Had

"That's him again on the other line. I'm not answering." Farren and Quinton resumed conversing the day after Li'l Marv was taken. Quinton seized this opportunity to get back in; but for Farren, Quinton was a warm body to talk to, not to take seriously. His attentiveness to listen to her gripes about Nasir, and how he didn't care about her, only his son, made him easy to communicate with.

"Don't. Make him sweat," Quinton persuaded her. "And you thought I was bad. This guy is taking you through it! Those chicks he messing around with ain't even on your level. Don't settle for anything."

"Right, like I settled for you," she ridiculed.

"I got a good job, my own car, and money in the bank. I'm not a hustla—that speaks loud enough about my character."

"All of that and you still live with ya momma! Letting her handle your affairs."

"My mom don't handle anything for me. I'm a grown-ass man."

"Then why was she meeting with my landlord, telling me you were interested in renting my place?"

"What are you talking about?"

"Ms. Lena said you were moving out and was looking for a place. Before all of this stuff went down, Nasir and I were moving to the suburbs, into a beautiful townhouse. I was giving up my place."

"Stop playin'! I'm not moving out until I have a $10 thousand dollar deposit for a house. I'm sure not renting, when I can live rent-free with my mom until I buy a house of my own."

"Why would your mom lie?"

"I don't know. Why don't you come over and ask her?"

Farren debated if she should go. A breath of fresh air would do her fine. She'd been cooped up for days, hiding away from the world.

"We don't have to stay here. We'll take a ride."

"Okay," she accepted. "I'm on my way."

Hssss!

Nakea entered her house with Li'l Marv on her hip and was greeted by clouds of smoke—weed smoke. Sean had a blunt in his mouth, dangling off to the side like a cigarette, with one foot on the floor and the other, on the tabletop; watching *Anaconda* with Ice Cube and Jennifer Lopez. Generally, the smoke wasn't bothersome, but under the circumstances, Nakea preferred her son be sleep when they blew trees.

"Shut the door, Kee, I've got something to show you."

Nakea situated her son on their bed, and in panic, rammed her back against the wall.

"What the fuck is that!" Her skin was crawling with fear.

"It's my baby. You have your son and I got mines!" Sean had a 12-foot, 100-pound army green, and black Burmese python, laying on the trim of the couch. "I won't fuck wit' yours and you don't fuck wit' mines, deal?" This wild snake was purchased off the street hot for $150, fifty percent off retail price. Unaware that the previous owner, an un-reputable breeder, got rid of it because it's growth potential could reach 20 feet, 200 pounds. At it current length and weight, the snake was already too much to deal with, so he sold it to the highest bidder: Sean.

The owner also failed to give him a sign of caution, and information that he needed a permit to carry this type of snake. Potential snake owners need to carefully research snakes before acquiring one. It is mandatory to have a secure escape proof enclosed tank. A licensed permit is required.

What he did offer Sean was a 55-gallon tank that was used for young, not adult, pythons. They required custom-built cages, modified by their size.

"You can't keep that in here!"

With limited resources and room for the snake, Nakea's complaint proved truthful. Why invest in a pet you can't maintain? Another important factor the previous owner left out, was that the snake needed to be fed every two weeks, not every three; but most importantly, he in haste for the sale, forgot to tell Sean the last time he fed the python.

"Did I tell *you* that, when you brought dat nigga's baby home for good?" he spit out in a jealous fit.

"Sean, he's my son!"

"Correction . . . he's a visitor that was made a permanent addition to our family."

A fear of Sean that she'd never known she had before, engulfed Nakea. Sure, the beatings and the gun incident let her know he was violent, but never did she know how many cold-hearted, multi-layered layers he possessed. This was not the young man she'd fell for years ago. This was a sour man that would go to any lengths to get those who betrayed him, and Nakea began to feel she was on that list.

"That snake has go to go . . . or else . . ."

Sean extended his arm for the 100-pound snake to slide on. He dropped a bit, then flexed his muscles to lever the extra weight. He rose the slimy snake's head to her face with its' black slim, dual-slit-tip tongue, darting in a out of it's mouth; hissing within inches of Nakea's lips. Pinned against the wall, Nakea dropped her head down as close as she could to her chest, not uttering a sound.

"Get used to this mafucka, 'cause it ain't goin' nowhere," he chattered through his teeth.

Nakea had to find a way to get Sean out of her life for good—her, and her son's lives were at stake. Not only did this snake urinate and defecate like a horse, but it ate like one as well.

Unless You're Invited—Stay the Hell Away!

Nasir and Brian had just finished bagging their product at their "business" apartment, and Nasir was heated. This was the last time Nasir would call Lena and she didn't answer. This time, he was in route to her house if she didn't pick up. Now he knew why she hadn't phoned. She had a new young boy: Chauncey. Jealousy wasn't settling in, it was the piece of information that Lena had used him, his body, and his soul. Stooping so low as to fuck her son's brother to get back at his mother.

Brian attached a backpack on his back, and hit the block.

"You cool, Nasir?"

"Yo, I'm fucked up! I might kill this bitch!"

Brian sat centered on the couch. "Which one? All ya bitches outta order." He had to joke to bring Nasir back to his senses.

"That bitch Lena!"

"Fuck her, man."

"It's not that simple. The bitch gotta pay for what she did."

"My concern is getting Chauncey and Sean—fuck her! Where are your priorities?"

"Yo, man, I didn't tell you Chauncey hittin' it?"

"Young ho, old ho, same ho's—all of them ho's, feel me?"

"I'm going over there."

"Dat nigga might be there. I'm goin' too." Brian went to the back to strap up, and placed a .22 in Nasir's hand."

"This firecracker ain't gon' do no damage. Lemme get my forty-five!"

ക്കക്കക്കക്കക്ക

Quinton was leaving the house after Farren rang the bell. Lena was curious what time he would return, so Chauncey could come through.

"What time will you be coming back, Q?" Lena asked, startled to see Farren; but internally smiled. "Hey, Princess."

Farren turned and said, "Hello," in a mild-mannered tone.

"I'm sorry to hear about your *third* miscarriage." Lena offered no real condolence. It was said neutrally, but made Farren feel like there was hidden contempt behind her words. "I'm ready when you are, Quinton." Thoughts percolated through her mind.

"Later, so don't wait up."

ໝ໑ໝ໑ໝ໑

In thirteen minutes flat, Chauncey showed up to dig old moms out. Like the slut she is, Lena prepared to turn him out. Chauncey parked his car in the same spot Quinton parked his. Nasir and Brian parked around the corner and walked through the alley that led to Lena's house, in a non-discrete manner. They neared the back of the house noticing the windows were up, allowing the summer breeze to blow through the screens. Nasir could hear Lena talking dirty to Chauncey.

The young boys were the bridge that connected her to yesterday—the days when she was in her prime. They kept her hot and energetic. Lena assumed that seductive, purring voice. Undoubtedly; it was all game. This was the same voice she used to seduce Nasir, which was now insulting and sickening to him, as he listened from the screen.

Nasir put one finger to his mouth to hush Brian from saying anything. Demons whispered in his ears. Chauncey benefited from Lena's snug walls that his muscle hooked. No matter how many men who had been up in there, Lena, did her kegel exercises, daily, to keep her muscles tight.

Afflicted in mind, Nasir rushed the door, kicked it in, and barged through the house to the back room, where Chauncey was putting a dent on the bedroom wall; chipping the paint from banging the headboard against it so hard.

Well Day'um!

Sonya strode—off the record—into Charter Elementary and demanded to speak with the HNIC— head nigga in charge. Dressed in a short-sleeved taupe skirt and a pair of dress slacks, she gave the presence of a working woman. Principal Hurdle escorted her to his office where he began listening to Sonya's formal complaint. She'd received a printout of Nasir's public records and produced photos that he'd taken in the past, with Chauncey on the block, hustling.

"This is the type of individual you have working for you in an educational environment," she spoke professionally.

"I see." He nodded. "We weren't aware of this." He stretched the truth a little to cover his own ass. He knew about the current cases, but not about this secret life.

"I am prepared to talk with the board of education, the Mayor's office, the Governor's office and to the press, if you don't terminate this employee. I'm convinced parents would love to learn that Charter Elementary hires child abusers," she beleaguered with urgency. Principal Hurdle gritted his teeth. Nasir put him in a problematic state of affairs.

217

"What can I do to stop you from going forward?" For a split second his pang of conscience distressed him.

"Fire him, today! Otherwise, the press will have this on the front page tomorrow."

"I understand your worry, but please allow us two days before you prematurely, drop the bomb."

"Deal." She stood up to shake his hand. "Mr. Hurdle, please don't underestimate me. If you keep him onboard, I will take it there," she warned him, shaking his hand firmly, before she departed.

Sonya is not to be fucked with. She poked her lips out, not regretting what she'd done in the slightest way.

Principal Hurdle left a message on Nasir's phone not to return, because the mustard was off the hot dog.

For a job that Nasir loved—making a difference in those boys' lives—he was torn between street life, and lust of the flesh; suffering enormously from the sins of his father.

Fetish

Chauncey had Lena's ass up high, sweating, while pounding her ass. "Real quick, do it now!" Lena begged. Chauncey released and squatted over Lena, who had lain flat on her back, and he grunted to release a long, dark brown turd—human feces. This was a first time, and a glorious moment for Chauncey—shitting on Nasir's old-head woman.

But when his bowel movement turned to a soft, slushy stool on Lena, compliments of old Chinese food from the neighborhood Wok restaurant, he was somewhat ashamed that he didn't have total anal muscle control. The room smelled of funk!

Nasir and Brian barged into the room, Chauncey dodged for his pants with fudge, covering his long chocolate pretzel. A dim ache penetrated through Lena, wickedly grinning at them.

"You dirty, bitch!" Nasir had his .45 directed at her. Caught in this kind of act, Chauncey was defiled. But how did they know he was there?

"Put some clothes on, you ass-lovin' mafucka," Brian hawked each movement of Chauncey's, as he put his pants on.

"Now, now, Nasir . . . let's not be childish about this. You got what you wanted—I got what I wanted!"

"You played me!"

"What's good for the goose is good for the gander! Don't bitch up now!" Unsmiling, Lena treated him like a punk.

Chauncey remained quiet under Brian's watch.

"You're just like your father—weak for pussy! Clap! Clap! Clap! You damn right, I played you to get back at that, bitch, Loretta! All of these years you ran these blocks while my son—*your* brother—didn't have any ties with the Bundy name."

Brian's heart jumped for Nasir, as he heard this devious woman spill out the truth. *Women ain't shit!* Brian thought.

"My son was Marv's first born—he should have been his namesake! Marv and Stan also had to pay. You think I fucked Freeze for no reason? Hell no! Bucky wasn't the real force behind him getting stabbed—I was! You think it was by chance Stan went to that motel when those tricks lied about getting their asses beat? Hell no! I set that up. And my way of paying back Loretta . . . the ultimate, fucking her son!"

All of this information, some new, although not connected at the time, revolved around Nasir's life. Riled with fear that he would be shot, Chauncey zipped for his gun, which was underneath his shirt, still lying on the floor. Brian saw him flinch and let a shot off, missing him, but hitting the vase on Lena's dresser. The last sentimental piece that Marv Sr. had given her, with his name engraved on the bottom it. It shattered to pieces. Weighted down in memory, Lena tussled to gather bits of the vase.

With the distraction of Lena's sentiment, Chauncey dropped to the floor, grabbing at Brian's legs. Nasir advanced toward them. Lena hurdled, slamming against Nasir's back. Chauncey broke free; bobbing and weaving the shots Brian fired, managing to let off a lucky shot himself.

The lack of restraint gave Chauncey the chance to run for the door.

In All Honesty

Francine met Loretta at her house. From what Stan told her, she had to finally reveal the truth. No more speculation, just the plain truth. To move forward with his future, Nasir had to build a relationship with his brother. But Francine was unaware of the ties that already bond them together. Poor timing for Francine; the news should've been spread years ago, but it was held back. She dealt with shoulda, coulda, woulda—it was really a spun web.

Disappointment took away from Loretta, leaving her high and dry. These were the end results. Loretta's life was one disillusion after another. Who was Francine to judge what she could or couldn't accept? And since no person lived the "ideal" life, Loretta had to face the setback during her inopportune times.

"Loretta sit down, I need to talk serious business." Francine wouldn't exaggerate the truth; it was time to keep it real. Loretta took a seat with a serious, worry-wrinkled face. "Nasir visited Stan, and explained *everything* to him."

"Everything like what?" she fired back for answers.

"About Lena."

"Tell me he did not tell my son about the possibility of her son being his brother!"

"It's not a possibility, Loretta . . . it's the truth. Let's face it."

"*Fuck* if it is true, Francine!"

"Loretta, they had a blood test done, and the boy is his. I went with Marv and the little boy to a private doctor—it's true!"

"I knew it! I knew it! You were fucking my man! I sensed you were a long time ago. You studied my moves and always wanted to be me!" Loretta released hidden, ill feelings that had been resting in her for years.

Francine shook her head and did not take this into account. "Get real, okay! I'm not even mad at you for your sick thinking. But to make it perfectly clear, I was doing it to protect *your* cuckoo ass!"

Loretta melted from the heat she was under. "Oh God, Francine!"

"What difference does it make now? These boys are grown and they need to know each other!"

Loretta wallowed from the bowels, "It matters because my son is fucking *that* boy's mother! I lived with whether or not that boy was Marv's child. Then, to learn from that hussy that not only did she have my man, but my baby boy too. To throw boiling water in my face, you confirm that you knew this all along? *Whose* friend are you? Where is the loyalty?"

Francine eased her bottom off the couch, adjusted her shirt, and parched her lips in disbelief of the news of Nasir having sexual relationships with Lena, then stated to her, "I believe that's a question your kids have been asking all these years . . . where is the loyalty?" Although Francine was disturbed by the final outcome, she didn't agree with Lena's behavior, but Loretta's were just as bad. Both had been mourning over 20 years for a man that was dead and gone. Neither of them mentally moved forward, and learned to cope by dealing harsh treatment toward others.

"As a friend, how can you sit up here and say that, when you know what I've been through?"

"Because, as a friend, I've been the one who stuck it out and weathered the storm with you, that's why I can say it." Clearly written all over Francine's face was concern. "We can get through this also." She opened to embrace Loretta, who accepted her warm embrace with hot tears.

Riverside Nursing Home

"Psst . . . Psst . . ." Bucky tried to quietly gain the attention of his buddy, Mitch. Mitch worked at the Riverside Nursing Home as an RN, but his primary job was dispensing medications to the residents. He was Bucky's inside connection for needles, Methadone and other painkillers that he could sell on the street, to get his own high.

With his peripheral vision, Mitch took a fleeting look at Bucky in the stairwell exit. He glimpsed to see if other nurses or clerks at the desk saw him as well. Expertly, he excused himself to chat with Bucky.

"You can't be popping up on my job. I told you I'd meet with you later."

"Lemme hold somethin', bay-bee." Buckets of sweat poured down Bucky's face; needing a boost for the day.

Mitch left him and came back with a few bottles of Methadone, and a few needles. "Here, take this and get gone!"

"Nurse . . . Nurse!" A resident from room 104 yelled.

"Damn! That bitchy-ass Bundy woman is a damn nuisance! It's time for her to take her meds."

"Bundy? Is she black or white?" The mention of the Bundy name made Bucky suspect. That name was one he'd never forget.

"She's black. Uh, Anna is her first name. She's a damn nuisance; always talking about her deceased son. Look, I have to go sedate her with these meds before she pitches a real fit."

It's a small world. Buck smiled.

He waited for Mitch to leave; making him think he was gone, but he wasn't. He had to check to see if Anna had anything worth stealing.

Marv had to leave her all his jewelry. All those rings he had. Bucky remembered.

When Mitch was down the hall in another patient's room, he sneakily tiptoed into Anna's room. Her glasses were off to the side, and the television was turned up a few notches to match her 30 percent loss of hearing.

"Is that my dinner?" she asked with a weary voice.

"Uh, no ma'am. It's uh . . . housekeeping." Bucky searched the closet where her personal belongings were, coming up short on an item of value to steal. "Broke ass," he muttered.

"What ya say?"

"Nothing, ma'am." On his last attempt to find something, he opened a drawer that held sentimental value to Anna: a framed photo of her son holding Nasir at the hospital. Bucky placed it under his shirt and peeped out the door—on his way to find a good nod.

Bye, Bye

"Are you coming wit' me?" Shonda purchased two plane tickets to Atlanta's Hartsfield airport on her way to visit with her girlfriend, Nicalett. The day had finally come and she'd received her housing voucher, but was told she had to find housing within 60 days, or she'd risk losing it. She got on the job promptly. Nicalett had scheduled three potential places for Shonda to see. Now Shonda was trying to persuade Nakea join her.

"Girl, I have to work. When you coming back?"

"Fuck dat job! And if I can help it—never! Pack all your stuff and let's go. What else is here for you to stay?"

"*I am!*" Sean charged in from the back door. "Her ass ain't goin' nowhere, but to work, and back home to me!" He gripped Nakea around her waist. "Ain't that right, Kee?" Nakea half-smiled.

"Don't front for him! I never thought I'd say this, but they say you will eat your words. Nasir was a better catch for you. This is one nigga you need to leave behind!" Shonda emphasized, staring Sean down.

"Shonda, don't play me like some punk ass nigga! You fuckin', hoodrat bitch!"

Li'l Marv and Mercedes, Shonda's daughter, were in the playpen, playing with alpha blocks. They were used to the loud voices.

"I call 'em as I see 'em. Only a punk-ass nigga carries a snake around his neck to intimidate people. It shouldn't even be in here with these kids."

The tank was on the floor in the living room, with a concocted cover Sean had on the top, for the "safety" of the children.

"One of those babies shit, go handle that and shut the fuck up!" he directed.

"I agree with Shonda." Trying to appeal to him, she said, "Boo . . . its in violation of my lease to have a pet. Plus, the big ass thing can burst open that homemade cover."

"Nakea, its Li'l Marv . . . he shit. Come change him." Shonda had her share of changing dirty diapers.

Sean removed the tank's cover, and placed the snake around his neck; walking around the house with no regard.

"Spiteful ass! And you thought Nasir was spiteful. He got the snake out 'cause he know we scared of it!" Sean looked at Shonda sideways, with his chin pointed to his right.

"What cha say?" The python's body covered Sean's arms and neck.

"Go the fuck 'head with dat nasty thing!" A horn blew. "That must be my taxi." Shonda's plane left in six hours, but it would take them 45 minutes to get to the airport.

"I thought *that* would shut you the fuck up!"

Nakea removed Li'l Marv from the playpen to change him. She had the baby wipes, pamper and the powder on the end table. Li'l Marv's two bottom teeth were cuttin' through. He had a rubber alpha block; chewing on it while Nakea readied to change him. She placed a towel under his buttocks, took out two baby wipes and cleaned his bottom. She placed the soiled pamper on the floor until she finished, to dispose of it.

"Damn, nephew, you hung like ya daddy," she said to piss Sean off. She kissed her sister on the cheek, then Li'l Marv, before saying goodbye as her and Mercedes left for Georgia.

A full minute had passed and Sean was still locked on Nakea's smile. He didn't find the humor in that at all. Snatching up the soiled pamper, he smeared it in her face. "This ain't no fuckin' game!"

Running to the bathroom, Nakea screamed within, *He has got to go!*

Sean went to cover up Li'l Marv with the snake still around his neck. He leaned over to get the clean pamper, and when he sat up to put it on him, Li'l Marv's pee spayed all in Sean's mouth.

AT THE COURT'S MERCY

You, little mafucka! He spit.

Clickity-Clack

"Move! Move!" Brian shouted, running out of Lena's house, shoving those in his way off the sidewalk, as Chauncey fled, continuing to let off shots. After Brian realized he was shot, he dipped behind a car, watching Chauncey make way, letting him think he escaped.

Back in the house, Nasir forcefully flipped Lena over, slamming her on the bed. She screamed in a high, shrieking pitch. His gun, in point blank range, was pointed in the middle of Lena's eyes—the present evil was gleaming in.

Coincidently, an old friend of Lena's passed through the commonly using the alleyway by her house, hearing loud voices being exchanged through an open window. Subconsciously, he slipped, without meaning to voice it aloud, "Lena?" he questioned.

Without stinting, Nasir forcefully pulled the trigger—*Boom!* That split second when she heard the "intruding voice," was all the time Lena needed to roll from the bed; dodging the bullet.

Not wanting to be identified by *that voice,* Nasir sprinted out the door in hot pursuit to catch up with Brian, and settle the unfinished business, running toward the car.

"Let's get outta here," he said charged, exchanging menacing stares with Brian whose arm had been grazed by Chauncey's lucky shot.

"That nigga shot me! It's a graze, but he was aiming to kill."

The emptiness that Nasir felt consumed him.

"Reload my shit! I'ma kill dis nigga!"

On The Block

With his ripped STOP SNITCHIN' shirt hanging flimsy off his shoulder, Chauncey demanded that Sean meet him on the block, expeditiously. His recruit obliged making certain that he had his boy-toy strapped on him.

"These niggas are gonna come through! I barely made it out that bitch!" He hyperventilated.

"Let's do dis!" Sean was ready to war.

◈◈◈◈◈

Bucky gloated in guilt, seeing happier moments with Marv Sr. and Nasir. The picture he stole from Anna made him sulk and reflect. After copping the Methadone, Bucky sold it to a recovering addict to by himself a bag of devil.

Sorry nephew, he strapped the belt around his arm securely, for his veins to pop out—praying that one would. Using his fingers from his free hand, he smacked away to make the vein appear. Out of the supply of needles he'd gotten from Mitch, he picked up a needle off the ground; in the alleyway between the houses on the block where Brian hustled. He pressed the far end of the needle to make sure air bubbles were out, found a vein and ejected the liquid poison into his body.

Loosening the belt on arm, his neck fell back in a nod. His arms and legs unresponsively felt invincible, as he had an outer body experience—he was in heaven. In the alley, his body relished being beside the picture of Marv and his nephew.

It takes no courage to get in the back of a crowd and throw a rock.

Thurgood Marshall

When the Lights Go Out

Sonya knew where to find the spare key to Chauncey's apartment; underneath the windowpane that was sealed with duct tape to keep water from seeping through, when it rained. It was the least suspected place a door key could be hidden.

It wasn't by coincidence that she discovered it. Chauncey sent her there to retrieve a case of bullets. The nine he had in his clip were used, and to win this war, he needed more. Yet, the small .22 would serve as backup protection, until Sonya came back with extra clips.

This spot was Chauncey's safe haven—no drugs, no paraphernalia were stashed there—and Sonya knew this. Never risking receiving fed time for drugs if they ran up in the house; he'd settle for a five-year gun charge. He could do a five piece standing up. That's what most, unleveled thugs thought, until they'd been hemmed up behind bars.

Chauncey was a thug of all thugs, living from house to house. His mother was openly gay with a man's presence; and her live-in lover, the soft and pink one of the duo, catered to the motherly duties. But this pair wasn't matched properly. Jealousy and rage ended this love affair in a murder-suicide, leaving Chauncey in the hands of whomever in the family willing to take him on.

Selling drugs was his avenue of getting money from the time he turned ten. That's why he was able to relate to the young boys like the Horsemen, who were in jail on indictments—Nasir and Sean. All of them at some point in their lives, lived through abandonment and distressing struggle.

Whether it was from the death of a parent or imprisonment. Both Sean's parents' were in jail on federal drug charges. However, whatever the condition, Chauncey would never tolerate un-loyalty. He lived by the code of the street, and if he had to take a life or two—it would set the tone—never betray Chauncey!

Sonya reached in her Rocawear pocketbook with gloves on, and pulled out 84 grams of crack; pushing it toward back of the plates in Chauncey's kitchen cabinet to conceal.

It's ova for him! I've been riding with dis nigga through it all—dropping dimes on niggas anonymously, from the payphone on the same block he hustles, and he gotta nerve to wear a STOP SNITCHIN' shirt like he ain't no snitch himself. When he's the reason his boys—the Horsemen, are jammed up! I threw cocktail bombs through people's windows, set niggas up, and dis nigga don't think I'm deserving of a three-karat diamond

*bracelet that I asked him to buy for me—a month ago—
for my birthday! Oh, he payin' for it . . . one way or
another!*

Committed to *not* one person, *but* herself, Sonya
successfully planted the crack in Chauncey's house.
Scheming, she carried out her revenge. Not getting a
tennis bracelet added to the extreme dislike she'd built
for the men, she chose to love. One by one, they used
and abused her, but it was time for them to get paid
back!

She received self-satisfaction from Nasir getting
fired. She hated that females she knew, who had sons
going to Charter Elementary, gave positive input about
Mr. B—that had to end.

*A man like Nasir could never be a role model. I'll
expose his ass first!* With malice in her heart, she used
public information to bring him down.

Now it was Chauncey's turn. The same payphone
he used to give anonymous tips on other hustler's in
the game, she planned to use to drop dime on him.

She withdrew the box of bullets from the location
Chauncey told her and smiled within. Shortly, he was
going down.

৶৶৶৶৶

Nightfall hit and the lack of streetlights on the
block, darkened the sidewalks.

"Be cool, don't start blastin' until you get a direct hit. I don't want stray bullets to take an innocent bystander. These bullets have Chauncey and Sean written on them." Brian was serious about putting them down. He was no killer, but that was before he'd been shot at. A fearful man behind the barrel of a gun is what he became when Chauncey fired on him. That itself, called for retaliation. The goal was to aim and kill. He began flowing with Young Jeezy and Akon:

I'll be on the block, wit' my thing cocked . . . yeah, 'cuz I'm a rider . . . I'm a sole survivor! If you lookin' for me you can find me on the block disobeying the law . . .

Nodding his head to the bass, Nasir got pumped with them.

"Let's ride, nigga!" Much like his father and Uncle Stan, Nasir and Brian were headed down the same path.

Running through shortcuts on the block, in route to scope it out, adrenaline rushed them on a death mission. Reaching the crosswalk, one alley separated them from destiny. Both men, darkly dressed, guns in hand, dodged in the alleyway agitated by a junkie nodded over. Brian used his gun to lift up the junkie's face.

"Fuckin' Bucky!"

Bucky's clouded, discolored, glossy eyes half-opened. The needle was still in his vein.

AT THE COURT'S MERCY

"Uncle Bucky?" Nasir questioned, apprehensively.

"Nephew." He smiled, releasing the needle from his arm.

"Get gone, Bucky; we about to light this block up!" Brian stepped over him, and Nasir cautiously moved out of the alley.

Bucky shook his face and stood to his feet, to give Nasir the picture of his father. Brian caught a glimpse of Sonya in front of Chauncey, but didn't see Sean, down by the stoop on alert, at the other end of the block.

"Oooo . . . www . . . oooo," Sean signaled to Chauncey. The war was on. The first shot to blast was from Sean's gun. He walked with confidence, blasting one shot after another. Nasir exchanged fire, but instead of going forth toward Sean, he backed up the block.

Sonya ducked down, sprinting out of the war zone. Others on the block rustled under cars, lying flat; praying that a bullet would whiz past them, not inside of them.

241

If a small thing has the power to make you angry, does that not indicate something about your size?
Sydney Harris

Can I Get One Bag?

Bones learned from Mitzy, one of her partying partners that Nasir was affiliated with B-right, and the crack they had was big and healthy in size. Mitzy told Bones, though she didn't smoke crack, where Bones could find Brian to cop. She had been copping off him now, for about a month.

Even though she lived on the opposite side of town, when she had the money to spend and a ride, she'd rather cop with Brian than in her neighborhood. Because the blast wasn't as good as the one she'd get from his rocks. Trying to get the best for her dollar, Bones made Tyaire accompanied her on the cop. Some dealers pitied kids being raised by addicts, and gave a little extra to get them off the block with their kids. Wretchedly, on this day, Bones and Tyaire ended up in the middle of the battlefield.

Bones had Tyaire underneath a car, scared straight.

"Keep still, Tyaire—don't move!"

Frightful tears ran down Tyaire's face. With Mr. B in sight, his fright toned down a bit.

"Mr. B! Mr. B!"

Nasir peered down to see Tyaire ease from under the car. Waving his hand, screaming, "Stay down!" Tyaire continued to rise for his protector to save him. Bones scraped her knuckles, seeing blood, desperately trying to pull her son back under the car.

Sean advanced forward. Nasir, seconds late, dove to shelter Tyaire, but his feeble body jerked twice, and blood shot out of his mouth as he called for Mr. B to rescue him, one last time. Nasir froze; body erect in distress. Tyaire arms were open, attempting to grasp onto Nasir's body.

Demon-filled thoughts in Sean's head, as he cocked back his gun.

Bucky held the picture close to his chest, determined to give it to Nasir. Coming out from the alley, his eyes beaded. Sean had a clear shot at his nephew, and just as Freeze had come to his rescue, he came to rescue for Nasir. Chastely, Bucky charged in the way of the traveling bullets that landed in his neck. As retribution, Bucky's faithfulness during the midst of the struggle, only accepted one evil thrust. But that one thrust took him out. Who would miss this dopefiend? Would anybody? The photo flew up in the air; landing next to Tyaire's wilted body.

Sean fired again. The other feral bullet pierced through Bucky, into Nasir's chest. Nasir reached forth, staring at the older image of him with heavy legs.

Through the turmoil, his body felt hot. A burning sensation permeated him, but he managed to smile. Sean stood overtop of him—face to face—head to head—with strong confrontation. Overcome with emotion and flooded with fear, was noticeable as Sean grasped the moment he dreamt of.

"Bitch-ass, nigga!" he reeked with demonic blood pumping in his veins. As if an ambush had taken him down, Nasir put one arm around Tyaire's unmoving body, the other on the picture of him and his father. With his eyes open, staring cockeyed at the gun between them, he thought of his son, as did his father, the day of his murder. *What would become of him now?* All he wanted to be was something he never had—a father.

Sean fired again, his hand shaking as blood shot back at his face. He left the three of them there— Tyaire, Bucky, and Nasir, and escaped from the area unharmed.

Bones' tears made a puddle underneath the car that protected her, watching in agony as Sean took each life, recognizing him as "the girl across the streets" man. To play hero was useless, her frail body fought against her, to find fat to absorb; she couldn't fight a bullet. When Sean hauled ass, she had a chance to come from under the car and grab the gun Nasir dropped, when he was shot.

On the other end, Brian's aim was off. Firing many bullets with only one hitting Chauncey in his hand. Once more Chauncey eluded death. But this time, Brian's pursuit wasn't over, until he was over. Chauncey weaved between cars as Brian wildly let loose bullets. In return, he fired back, but didn't have enough time to grab of the both clips Sonya brought to him, only one. Sparingly, maybe two bullets were left. So he had to preserve those in case the situation got tighter. If he could make it to his house, he'd be fine. Plenty of bullets were in there.

Reaching the front door of his crib, he slammed hard into the door to get him; Sonya still had his keys. Brian was seconds behind him. Officers in unmarked cars dashed for both of them.

Sonya huddled over Nasir and with a rebel yell she called out his name, *"Nasir!"* Never did she want him taken out. Shaken up, yes, but not shaken away. The sound of her cries stung her heart. Both she and her mother shared a common memory for the name, Marvin Bundy.

While we are mourning the loss of our friend, others are rejoicing to meet Him behind the veil.
John Taylor

Long Time, No See

Loretta walked into the reception room of the Riverside Nursing Home with an engineered smile.

"Sign in here, please," an Indian woman with a black Bindi, an eye-arresting, blazing round symbol of good fortune, on her forehead, asked gracefully, "Who are you coming to visit?"

"Anna Bundy, room one hundred and four."

"Oh, Mrs. Anna," dreadfully, she warned her. "She just had her meds, so she may be a little out of it."

Loretta kept her mouth in check. However, when she entered the room, Mrs. Anna triggered flashbacks.

"Marvin?"

"No, Mrs. Anna, it's me, Loretta."

"Loretta?" She checked her memory bank. "Baby, how you been? Marvin just left here. He'll be right back; I'm sure he'll be happy to see you!"

"Oh," Loretta dazed. "I'm making it."

"Tell the truth and shame the devil!" Mrs. Anna was curled up under her covers.

"But barely," Loretta added. "I can't seem to shake these dreams—well . . . nightmares I keep having of Marv.

"Me either, baby; he's always coming to see me."

"How do you deal with it?"

"What you mean? That's my son; we have great conversation!"

"Oh."

"Submit to him and you'll be all right. The dreams won't be nightmares anymore, but precious times with him."

Loretta smiled.

No man can think clearly when his fists are clenched.
George Jean Nathan

Can I live?

Lena had just pulled up, determined to visit Mrs. Anna. Before she could exit the car, she spotted Loretta coming out the front entrance. She sat dispassionate, sweat dripping from her nose. She used one hand to wipe the sweat away and the other to cover her face. The closer Loretta came, the more cautious she became. This woman scorned would go to the depths, in lack of consideration for others. In the process, she didn't care who got hurt—who it affected—as long as she was gratified.

The crucial information of Anna's whereabouts hand been snowballed out of Bucky. She'd seen him and his white friend, and he contently let her know in exchange for some green, that he'd seen her son's grandmother over at Riverside Nursing Home. What better place to pursue peace than an old folks home?

The car Loretta came in exited the parking lot. Lena pounced out the car wearing a straw hat and dark glasses. She whipped past the unoccupied visitor's desk as the on staff person left, temporarily, to use the bathroom. Those on the unit where Anna's room was, assumed that Lena was signed in. Lena read each door, stopping at room 104. Anna was very relaxed, and thankful that Loretta came to see her. Visitors for her were scarce. With her bad eyesight, she thought it was Loretta who had come back in.

"Loretta, baby, you back so soon?"

Lena altered her voice, disguising the pain she felt for years from this woman. She'd taken Quinton over her house many times hoping for acceptance, receiving none.

"I left my bag behind the door."

"Okay, baby."

Lena softly pushed the door to close, and turned the lock-latch securely. "I'm just gon' close the door a bit so I can reach it." She came closer to Anna who was watching one of her favorite movies—*Car Wash*. Removing her hat and glasses, Lena sat on the bed with a confused Anna.

"You're not my daughter-in-law!"

Lena smiled as she leaned in. "Oh, yes I am!" She snatched one of the pillows under Anna's head and placed it over her face, pitilessly smothering her. Anna's weak, fragile body barely moved with the kicking of her feet. Lena held the pillow down until the kicking stopped, and Anna's body was unyielding. With the satisfaction of taking her life, Lena put her hat and glasses back on, unlocked the door, and with poise, she walked out of the room.

She drove back to her house relieved that finally, there was retribution.

෯෯෯෯෯

Inside of Lena's house, Farren was saying her final goodbyes to Quinton. The evening was pleasant, but still, she needed to bring closure with Nasir, before she engaged in another relationship. More over, she hadn't erased the bad memories of their courtship.

"Thank you for being a friend, Quinton. Tonight was entertaining."

"Stay over with me. Let me hold you all night."

"Nice thought, but no thanks. I really need to talk with Nasir."

Hearing Nasir's name alerted Lena. "Who's in the bedroom with you, Quinton?" A tight sensation elated more mental anguish.

"Really, it's time for me to go." Farren said, colliding with Lena's question as they walked out the room together.

Lena waited outside her bedroom door. "It's you!" Disgusted, she spat, dejecting Farren.

Sparks went off, with Quinton ensnared by his mother's response. "Mom, what's your problem?"

"Her!" Lena tossed aside her hand, pointing to Farren's face.

"Me?" Totally absorbed, Farren frowned.

"Princess, you are clueless. Wrapped up in your little world, a mommy and daddy's li'l girl. A bomb could be in your face and you wouldn't run!"

"Excuse me?!" Farren twisted her head from the mist of saliva coming from Lena's mouth.

"Mom!" Quinton trembled with shame.

"Don't mom me!" Lena had finally gone over to the mentally challenged side. Her mind was gone. "I fought for you to have a normal life, trying my best to bring you closer to the family you never knew. The closest I came was to your brother . . . Marvin Bundy, Jr., a.k.a. Nasir! And after all of that, both of you were fuckin' the same woman!"

Quinton was speechless. He'd only known Nasir, by Nasir, never his full name.

Farren was numb. "Nasir's your brother?" Breathlessly, her ticking pulse ceased.

Shuttering, Quinton searched for the right words, but failed to find them. "My brother?" At that moment, he craved to find more to say.

Cascaded, Lena ground out savagely, "Your *brother—her* man—that *I* fucked!"

Grappling at her chest, Farren's heart was kidnapped and she had yet to find it. Lena volunteered this information for several reasons, but the main reason—to expose what had been sweep under the rug for years.

This construed confession chased after Farren, who'd darted out the house. Her eyes could not see, but her ears heard the lust of the flesh.

The rivalry illuminated the calmness of Lena's voice as she tried to reason with her son, why she'd gone this far. Uninvited, he bombarded his way in his mother's bedroom. The deepest secrets spawned the evil in individuals. Lena's shadow of darkness hovered over her for over twenty-one years. Quinton, up to this point, hadn't an ill thought about his mother. But with the truth revealed, her dual personalities were exposed. Figuratively, he strangled her with words of death.

"I curse *God* for the day you were born!" He walked out of his mother's life, without the possibility of tomorrow. Lena found a thrill in thriving off of everyone's misery except her own. She wore so many faces to get the job done. Acting "as-if" to everyone.

Farren's tears drizzled from her face for both of her loves—one a blessing, one a curse! That briefly summoned up the reason why Lena's company made her uncomfortable. Their spirits didn't agree. Did Nasir really have sex with her? Was Lena telling the truth? Satanic spirits don't backstab; they stabbed you in the heart to witness the agonizing pain—Lena had that spirit.

Farren had yet to endure that agonizing pain, until she turned down a block that the police had taped off. Onlookers were gauging their heads in sorrow. Aroused interest got her out the car, not knowing what lay ahead.

She timidly halted by Sonya's ferocious screams. If she heard her right, it was Nasir's name Sonya was yelling out. Farren's pace changed from peak interest to a need-to-know basis of the bodies that were chalked. The muscles around her eyes began twitching as she came closer. Stopped by an officer and stalled, she scooted around him, struck by the sight of Nasir's body, and two others that were dead. Badly affected by what she saw, Farren fainted. Would she ever find love again? Or, would she become the next Loretta?

Dreams are today's answers to

tomorrow's questions.

Edgar Cayce

Can the church say Amen?

A missionary from the Tabernacle of Faith Holy Temple, Sister Regina, was making her rounds to check on elderly members of the congregation. When Mom Flossy came of age, she joined so when her day came—she'd be saved. Besides that, she didn't attend; but once in awhile, she'd watch the television broadcast of the service on the local channel.

"Mom Flossy?" Sister Regina hollered through the mail slot in Mom Flossy's door.

"The door is unlocked, Regina, come in," she answered, recognizing her voice.

Regina let herself in. "God laid it on my heart to check on you. We haven't seen you at any of the services this month and you missed the "Come In Alive" revival. God moved in that place! We had a Holy Ghost time. The anointing was heavy." Sister Regina gave praise.

"Was the spirit up in that place?" Mom Flossy teased, but Regina was only telling what she saw.

"Pastor was laying hands and people were getting slain in the spirit!"

"Shut yo' mouth!"

"Jesus is real!"

"Yes, *He* is!"

"I wanted to obey the Lord, so I came soon as *He* laid it on my heart. Is there anything I can do for you?"

"Well, it would be nice if you could carry me over to my daughter's house. I asked my grandbaby, but she's busy and I haven't seen my grandson this evening."

Sheena really told her, "No, Grandmom. I can't deal with her right now."

"God told me to bless you. Of course I'll take you, but can it wait until tomorrow morning? It's awfully dark."

"No, I don't think so, just like God laid it on your heart, *He* laid it on mines."

"Amen! The Word of God says that when two or more agree . . . so, I'll take you there since its God's will."

"Reach my walker for me," Mom Flossy used her weight on the arm of the couch and pulled up. "I'll need it to get up her three steps. Her place is not handicap accessible like mine. My wheelchair can't skip up steps." She giggled with Sister Regina.

"Well, I'll get you up and over those steps. God has our back! Amen!"

"Amen to that!" Mom Flossy animated her.

Sister Regina assisted Mom Flossy in the church van. Placing her wheelchair and walker in the back, and then they set off to Loretta's.

ঔ঺ঔ঺ঔ঺ঔ঺ঔ঺

In the middle of the floor, Loretta had a bottle of Knottyhead—Seagram's Gin, chuckling, listening to the Isley Brothers' *Between the Sheets*, and having a one-sided conversation. But she believed Marv was talking back to her.

"Stop that," she playfully giggled. "That tickles. Keep on and I'ma put it on you." Pissy drunk, she guzzled straight from the liquor bottle.

"Huh, oh you want it, do you? I'll show you!"

With her knees planted in the linoleum floor, her body wobbled to get balance. One knee spread further than the other, and her legs expansively collapsed like the flaps of a butterfly. Loretta fell over laughing.

"I'm fucked up, Marv, ain't I? Here, take this Knottyhead. I can't drink no mo' of it." She passed the gin; and sat it right beside the 18 x 24-sized poster she had framed of her and Marv.

Early, when she visited Anna, the bit of sense she was holding on to became truant. Peeling layer after layer of clothing off, Loretta was fully nude.

"How you want it, baby?" She turned her backside to the picture, turned her head over her shoulder and began shaking her cellulite-covered ass. She took one hand and started spanking her ass cheek. "You like it when I shake it, don't you?" Then, she began to grind her hips. "No, you like it when I double-pump even more!" Her tongue was dangling out the side of her mouth as she waved her body, skipping clumsily to the poster frame. "Let's make a baby." Her arms cuddled the contour of the frame as she used her tongue to lick the glass that had dust and old stains on it.

৶৶৶৶৶

Sister Regina and Mom Flossy had rung the doorbell three times. Loretta hadn't responded, but they knew she was in there; they heard her voice over the music.

"Turn the knob, Regina." Mom Flossy clasped to maintain her steadiness with the walker.

"It's not of God to enter in the presence of those of sin."

"In the name of Jesus, will you stop being such a holy-roller! Turn the *damn* knob!"

The music and laughter cautioned Sister Regina that partying was going on.

"God wouldn't bring us this far to leave us," she said a silent prayer.

As instructed, she turned the knob and it was unlocked. She pushed gently for Mom Flossy to step inside. Once in, neither of them expected to see Loretta in such a condition.

"*My Lord!* Satan, the Lord God rebukes you! The blood of Jesus is covering this place!" Sister Regina began to recite the Lords prayer: *The lord is my Shepard, I shall not want* . . .

Mom Flossy didn't need an illustrated picture; she had the original scene, live. "My child is a basket case," she snuffled, then loudly, over the music, commanded Regina to call for help.

Loretta had to be admitted—not to the hospital, but a facility that catered to the mentally ill. Making out with a photo frame and reminiscing; she wasn't all there, and she was haunted by Marv's spirit.

We must constantly build dikes of courage to hold back the flood of tears.
Dr. Martin Luther King, Jr.

Mistreated

Misled by the perception that Sean loved her, Nakea began to see the spontaneous expressions and changes that he'd taken her through. Feeling abandoned and mistreated, yes . . . she'd join Shonda in Atlanta, but not until housing was in place. Until then, she'd keep her job, take care of her son and wait it out patiently.

Li'l Marv was cranky again, his bottom teeth cutting in bothered him, and he gnawed on any object he could. Nakea ate most of the chicken on the drumstick, before giving it to her son to chew on. Before going near the television, she glanced at the snake's tank—it was gone.

Whew! I'm glad he took that nasty thing out of here.

Carefully, she pre-cautioned, before turning on the tube—the remote was lost. She hit the on button, occasionally looking out of her front window, as she usually did when she was watching TV. She peeped out, watching Shanira walk back and forth in front of her house with two girls.

What's this ho about to do?

Nakea journeyed to the front door, double-checking on her son before she went out front. Li'l Marv was biting away, content with his chicken bone. Down the steps she walked, with one hand on her hip.

"Hey, what's up with you, Shanira?"

Shanira purposely created a scene to stir drama with Nakea. They were cool, but they weren't that cool. The two girls with Shanira provoked her.

"Fuck it! I'll say somethin'."

Shanira snickered nervously. "You called welfare on me 'cuz I fucked yo' baby daddy?" With a glancing blow, Shanira had Nakea's complete attention. This was a time she warranted Shonda's attendance. She'd cuss them out and hit all three of those young chickens.

Nakea squinted. "You got the wrong one. First off . . . I wouldn't do no shit like that. Second off . . . your problem is with Farren—not me; *that's* Nasir's woman!" Cleary, Shanira came to fight. In the projects, you never stepped foot to another woman's domain with confrontation, unless you were ready to throw bows, or kick a fair one.

Li'l Marv lost grip of his chicken bone, swatting the playpen, whining for it.

As a scare tactic Sean let the snake roam free before he left. Searching for a meal—hungry—it slithered behind the playpen. It hadn't been fed in three weeks. The last meal was digested and long passed through its' system. It had an acute sense of smell for food—rats, mice, rabbits, and chicken.

The smell of the chicken setoff a feeding frenzy. That, along with the violent tapping, nerved the wild snake. Raising high, sloping down into the playpen, the snake winded his body from the baby's feet to his torso, to his neck, ultimately covering his body.

While Nakea was outside pleading her case, the wild python was using its strength to wrap tight, and squeeze the innocent breath out of this child; causing a circulatory arrest. No blood was present in Li'l Marv's neck, or in the middle of his torso. The baby was desperately struggling—gasping for air, coming up void—with nothing, but agonal breathing—suffocation. The python with a girth the size of a telephone pole, squeezed its' helpless small being: the precious, tender essence of life; the exuberant, happy life of a young, sweet, loving baby. Not being fed triggered instinctual behaviors, and Li'l Marv became its' prey.

What Sean didn't realize, that the previous owner did, was no matter how tame and friendly a Burmese Python can be, they will always be wild animals; unpredictable in behavior.

Nakea's negotiations with a go-getting, chickenhead, over her baby's daddy, ceased. She wasn't arguing with this broad anymore. To fight her was useless; to continue arguing when she had heavier issues on the brain—useless! Being the bigger person for once, she walked back up the same steps she came down, opened the front door, and her motherly instincts kicked in full gear.

Li'l Marv's limp body stretched out in the playpen. The snake let him go and prepared to swallow its' prey. Opening its' unrestrained jaws, showing its' maxillary and platine teeth, he began sucking down his legs. Nakea's heart moved from her chest to her throat. She refused to believe what was about to occur.

Afraid, but protecting her flesh and blood, she, in a flash grabbed the machete in the corner of the kitchen where Shonda left it. With the snakes body, half in and half out, she went into attack. Swinging wildly, chopping the lower end of the snake.

Nakea's tears burned her face as her heart shredded into pieces. With every bit of life ignited inside of her, she alerted neighbors 30 miles away with her penetrating, cutting pitch of grief.

Without recourse, seeing her son lay there breathless, she axed the snake in clusters. Snake blood squirted; flying and spilling on the walls and. Standing ten feet high, the snake unloosed Li'l Marv and rose up for attack. The movement of its eyes upwardly met hers.

Pursuing what it started, it jolted to wind around Nakea, but with all her might and the sharpness of the machete, she sliced the head of the snake's body off, screaming for dear life. The rest of its' body wiggled from side to sides going through the physical motions, until it eventually, dropped and stopped.

Remorseful guilt contained Nakea and she consoled the body of her breathless baby boy. She cradled him, running to a corner free of blood, sitting shell-shocked. Her body trembled as she attempted to administer CPR to resuscitate him. She pumped on his chest cavity, hoping to jumpstart his heartbeat.

"Oh God!" she screamed, casting the demons to hell. "He's breathing! He's breathing!" She smiled of joy, but covered it with saddened tears, when she realized it was her imagination. Tears of despair, matched with shattered screams filled this mother's temple. The loss of her first born—her only child; her only son; never to be seen after burial—on the account of a "God" complexed, selfish, pathetic, inconspicuous, cowardly, jealous man, who didn't love her, but only the way he could control her. If she trusted her instinct in the beginning, the truth was, she'd never be in this horrible predicament. However, tragedy has no preference.

People outside on the block, gathered around. By the sounds coming from Nakea's house, they knew it was grim, whatever it was.

AT THE COURT'S MERCY

The same feeling compelled Bones. Only a mother that's lost a child knew of this pain.

With the door left open, Bones entered the house with bits and pieces of the snake, and puddles of blood. The scene spoke volumes without words—death. Bending awkwardly, an impulse that Bones never had felt before—to kill, came over her. This man—Nakea's man—was responsible for the death of her son and Nakea's son. Clumps of snake was scattered about, letting her know what transpired.

For stable support, the sanity on her face showed she was concentrating on what to do. And then, the power-presentation of her own sons' smile made her take Nasir's gun, and place it by Nakea's side. Looking into each other's eyes was like looking into a room with nobody there. Bones lowered her eyes; premonition of tears.

Tables can turn; you never know when you need somebody. Bones, a.k.a. the crackhead of the block, left Nakea the gun—Nasir's gun—to pursue the death mark: Sean.

We cannot banish dangers, but we can banish fears. We must not demean life by standing in awe of death.

David Sarnoff

Dooms Day

The throw-down and escape from the scene of the crime changed Sean's pace. Now he could relax, Nasir was out of their lives for good! Never did he have to worry about Nakea leaving him for him, again. His adrenaline had subsided at this time of night. As he approached home, he investigated the house closer, wondering why practically every light was on. Why the shades were still up and not down.

Nakea hadn't moved since the heinous act, cradling her son—unforgiving. Waiting for Sean to enter—it was lights out for him!

From where Nakea sat, cattycorner to the door, Sean would see her. He jogged up the stairs yelling, "Yo, Kee!" Such images as the ones he saw were the actions of Nakea's emotions and reactions. There was nothing to laugh about. He studied her without movement, voiceless from site the blood and severed snake parts. Li'l Marv lay in her arms, but his head hung, without muscle support. Nakea's emotions hit quicker than his, but hers weren't limited to facial expressions like his were, most were hidden within.

Indifferent to what he had to say, with a tender heart, Sean apologized, "Kee, I'm truly sorry!" He came nearer, begging and pleading to her. Nakea needed little provoking to take him out. The scream she let out—printed in her memory.

With Nasir's gun mobilizing her energy, her brow furrowed and she ferociously aimed and shot three times—the gun rattling loudly. Her heart swelled painfully, presiding over her fear of him. A film of perspiration mixed with her tears—an emotional low— at her most vulnerable time, she wished her li'l pookie had stayed with Nasir. Was it worth her having custody now? That would forever playback in her mind.

Special Note to the Reader

We share a common interest, African American literature. From the heart, I thank you for following the "Unsympathetic Villain with a Pen's," literary career. ☺ You ask—I deliver. So with that, know, I didn't leave you stranded on an island. This time, I threw thousands of life preservers to bring all of you to shore.

Without further ado, let's open the doors together; take a seat in the pews and watch . . . *At the Court's Mercy.*

Until next time,
Precioustymes

One Love, One Spirit,
KaShamba

Remember, time is precious, never waste it on negativity!
KaShamba Williams

At the Court's Mercy

Present day pictures of previous judges were nailed on the wood paneled Superior courtroom wall. Five flags hung with pride—the stand out—the United States flag trimmed with gold-braided roping. Eager bailiffs seated family members and friends, before the trial began. Nakea sat quiet as the silent clock moving its' shaky arm. The first row of hard wooden seats, sat in back of the steel gate that separated the employees, families and criminals. Teary-eyed, Daisy, Nakea's mother, and Shonda, hoped for the best possible outcome for her.

Nakea was in the courtroom that offered merciless, stiffened penalties for coming to court late. One bailiff explained to another defendant; a capias was already issued for him showing up *one* minute late. The young man's face turned from complacent to duress instantly. He handed a rubber banded wad of money that he had in his possession to his mother, in fear the courts would seize it, and was promptly escorted past the silver gate that protected staff—he was off to detainment. They were not playing!

Nakea heard the call for Nakea Perkins, case number, 41705 on the docket. Her body felt a chill.

The hair rose from her arms, and her ears seemed to enlarge, igniting the whispers of those in the courtroom. People stared down the bench, eyes darting around other, giving Nakea hardened looks. Court officials whirled around the chairs and joked amongst each other, as this was an ordinary day for them; not the least bit riddled with guilt, as the criminal offenders waited their turn to face the judge.

Judge Francowski tapped on the mouse of his computer, dressed in his black steamed-out robe of honor, waiting for Nakea to stand trial. He was very precise with strictness, adhering to the courts' sentence guidelines.

The lighting in the courtroom could stand some brighter bulbs. It was gloomy enough facing a murder charge. It made for a better situation, but it didn't for those that worked there. The butterflies in Nakea stomach were a constant reminder of what was about to unfold.

Nakea's attorney, the one who Farren had asked to defend as a favor for her mother, Leslie, who worked as a litigation specialist for the top lawyers in town, argued back and forth in Nakea's defense.

Though Farren was heartbroken, she wasn't heartless. Yes, Nakea took her through uncalled-for drama, but *no* woman deserved to witness the death of a child. If she didn't know, she did now. . . that fate was real.

Added to that, finding out the father of her child was murdered by her live-in boyfriend, *that* contributed to Farren's softness of heart to help her. No, Farren never peeped a word to her; they were not friends.

The anguish of losing a loving father, a half-groomed, well-on-his way to becoming a good man, broke down that pettiness. Getting Nakea a lawyer was only right, because had Farren never left the baby in the house alone, he'd still be in Nasir's custody—both of them alive.

Nakea tried to remain in the appropriate posture that her lawyer instructed her of, but her arms kept folding, signaling to the judge that she was closed to what he was ruling. She looked back to her mother and Shonda, mostly Shonda, against the lawyer's wishes.

Quickly, she turned back, loosened up, and unfolded her arms. She stood upright with her arms rested on her sides, in an attentive stance. Solemn tears ran down her face; her case made major headlines. Surely, this case would be used for future reference. Superior Court vs. Nakea Perkins. Case number 41705.

You're not getting digits—only letters—Life! Evil thoughts plagued Nakea's mind. Waiting on her fate, one last time she looked back, this time, to the other side where Sheena, Mom Flossy, Francine, Farren and Bones, also waited to hear the outcome. Was justice served—a life for a life? Were there regrets?

Here she was prepared to speak on her behalf and the judge would determine her fate by the knock of a gavel. Cold as ice, and as immoveable as steel that under girthed America's bridges, were the hearts of the "powers that be"—that held the future of her life in their hands.

Nakea closed her eyes, then opened them wide— only seeing "the ruler," the "final decision maker" before her—Judge Francowski, who officiated and read the conclusion of her case.

"Nakea Perkins, the court finds you . . . guilty. However, we accept the plea of temporary insanity. Therefore, you have been sentenced to five years on the charge second-degree murder," the judge announced, placating his conscience.

Applause erupted and low chatters filled the courtroom. Other than Nakea, Shonda was really relieved that her sister didn't have to spend the rest of her young life in prison. In five years, she'd come and live with her in Decatur, Georgia, where she'd found housing.

Stop Snitchin'

Afraid, now that he was locked up, facing 25 years—for guns and drugs, Chauncey pondered if the Horsemen, whom were in the same prison, had read the transcripts with name on it, snitching on his crew to avoid jail time.

Today was his first day in general population so, he'd find out. The cellblock he was temporarily housed on was cell block G, the next tier over from cell block H. Both of the tiers, Stan had on lockdown.

To gain knowledge, the Horsemen became acquainted with old man Stan, the OG of his day.

"One important rule to the game—if you ever get caught—never snitch on the next man! Be a man, and accept the position you played." Stan would school them.

Chauncey walked down the tier, seeing three of the Horsemen.

"Yo kid, what up?" He was greeted with love.

Seriously relieved, Chauncey greeted them back, "What up, niggas?"

"Check it, we gon' help you get settled in. Here, take a few bags of these chips, a couple of candy bars, a few of these cup of noodles, and you should be straight until your commissary builsd up. We know ya ass hungry." One of the Horsemen persuaded him to come inside a cell.

Chauncey smiled, rubbing his stomach for some grub. He was hungry as hell! But when he walked inside, he walked directly into a death trap. They immediately went to work, repeatedly stabbing him with a homemade shank—a sharp object.

"Dat's for snitchin', mafucka! Snitches don't get stitches in here . . . they get taken out!"

One of them spit on him, "Dat's for Nasir, nigga! He was a thorough dude!"

Stan had the power to call the young men off of him, but why would he? Chauncey violated the rules! Besides, he had Brian, a.k.a. B-Right to groom into a real man for the next 10 years, which was the sentence he was given.

Many will stand before a judge in a court of law to determine the fate of their lives, but all will stand before God, and the wrath is always greater!

Hold Up, Wait a Minute!

Sheena was keeping her grandmom, company. They were sitting on the enclosed porch, reminiscing about Nasir and Loretta. Although Sheena's relationship with her mother never evolved, it pained her to see her confined—tied down in that awful stained, white strait-jacket.

After Mom Flossy made Sister Regina make "that call," she asked her to call Francine and Sheena, because she still hadn't gotten a hold of Nasir.

When they learned of Nasir's murder, all of them— Mom Flossy, Sheena and Francine—were staked with pain. But with the support of each other, they'd make it through. As for Bucky's death, only Mom Flossy deeply mourned the loss of her first born.

They made frequent visits to see Loretta with hopes of jarring her sanity, but Loretta still mumbled and talked to her imaginary partner— Marv, not them.

৯৯৯৯৯

Sonya wobbled her way up Mom Flossy's ramp, six months pregnant. A drop was all it took to knock her up. Unlike her mother, she wouldn't just have memories; she'd be blessed with having Nasir's baby.

"Who's that?" Grandmom Flossy slowly voiced.

"It looks like—uh, un . . ." Sheena grunted. "Like—Sonya!"

Sonya could see the shocked expressions on their faces. "Hey, Sheena, and Mom Flossy! Guess what? I'm six months pregnant with Nasir's baby and *this time*, I'm keepin' it! If it's a boy, I'm naming him, Marvin Bundy the fourth, so the name can live on!"

Sheena put her hands in her face and dropped to her lap yelling, *"Nasir! Damn you!"*

Mom Flossy rocked back and forth, shaking her head. "That's my grandson—in the image of his father, always thinking with the wrong head!" Then she mumbled, "And the cycle continues."

Change is Gonna Come

Lena, who thought she'd gotten off easy, was arrested three weeks after she murdered Anna Bundy. Riverside Nursing Home had her on closed circuit cameras that were placed in each room. The man that identified her: Mitch. He remembered her as the woman that Bucky gave information to for a few bucks.

ૹૹૹૹૹૹ

Tyaire, an innocent child caught by the bullet, had his most important wish in the world answered—his mother, Bones, stopped getting high and became an advocate; fighting laws that permit snakes as pets. What she saw that day, nobody else should ever see.

ૹૹૹૹૹૹ

Farren, with the help of her mother and father, sought out counseling to help stabilize her mind once again. Finishing her classes at the community college, she graduated in the spring.

After graduation, she had plans of moving to California, going to UCLA for graduate school, to embark on a career in Psychology. Having her share of mental problems, Farren figured it was time that she helped others deal with theirs.

IN STORES NOW

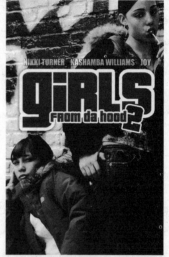

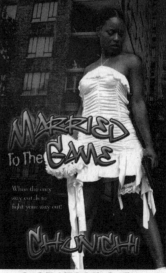

urban books presents

Urban Affair

a novel by
Tony Lindsay

1-893196-27-5

Scandalous
The Church Will Never Be The Same!

a novel by
ReChella

1893196-30-5

URBAN BOOKS PRESENTS
PAY BACK

a street saga by
roy glenn

FEBRUARY 2006
1-893196-37-2

URBAN BOOKS presents
HARLEM CONFIDENTIAL

COLE RILEY

FEBRUARY 2006
1-893196-41-0

MARCH 2006
1-893196-32-1

FEBRUARY 2006
1-893196-39-9

MARCH 2006
1-893196-33-X

APRIL 2006
1-893196-34-8

OTHER URBAN BOOKS TITLES

Title	Author	Quantity	Cost
Drama Queen	LaJill Hunt		$14.95
No More Drama	LaJill Hunt		$14.95
Shoulda Woulda Coulda	LaJill Hunt		$14.95
Is It A Crime	Roy Glenn		$14.95
MOB	Roy Glenn		$14.95
Drug Related	Roy Glenn		$14.95
Lovin' You Is Wrong	Alisha Yvonne		$14.95
Bulletproof Soul	Michelle Buckley		$14.95
You Wrong For That	Toschia		$14.95
A Gangster's girl	Chunichi		$14.95
Married To The Game	Chunichi		$14.95
Sex In The Hood	White Chocalate		$14.95
Little Black Girl Lost	Keith Lee Johnson		$14.95
Sister Girls	Angel M. Hunter		$14.95
Driven	KaShamba Williams		$14.95
Street Life	Jihad		$14.95
Baby Girl	Jihad		$14.95
A Thug's Life	Thomas Long		$14.95
Cash Rules	Thomas Long		$14.95
The Womanizers	Dwayne S. Joseph		$14.95
Never Say Never	Dwayne S. Joseph		$14.95
She's Got Issues	Stephanie Johnson		$14.95
Rockin' Robin	Stephanie Johnson		$14.95
Sins Of The Father	Felicia Madlock		$14.95
Back On The Block	Felicia Madlock		$14.95
Chasin' It	Tony Lindsey		$14.95
Street Possession	Tony Lindsey		$14.95
Around The Way Girls	LaJill Hunt		$14.95
Around The Way Girls 2	LaJill Hunt		$14.95
Girls From Da Hood	Nikki Turner		$14.95

Girls from Da Hood 2	Nikki Turner		$14.95
Dirty Money	Ashley JaQuavis		$14.95
Mixed Messages	LaTonya Y. Williams		$14.95
Don't Hate The Player	Brandie		$14.95
Payback	Roy Glenn		$14.95
Scandalous	ReChella		$14.95
Urban Affair	Tony Lindsey		$14.95
Harlem Confidential	Cole Riley		$14.95

Urban Books
74 Andrews Ave.
Wheatley Heights, NY 11798
Subtotal: _____
Postage:_____ Calculate postage and handling as follows: Add $2.50 for the first item and $1.25 for each additional item
Total: _____
Name: _____
Address:_____
City: _____ State: _____ Zip: _____
Telephone: ( ) _____
Type of Payment (Check: ___ Money Order: ___)
All orders must be prepaid by check or money order drawn on an American bank.
Books may sometimes be out of stock. In that instance, please select your alternate choices below.

Alternate Choices:

1._____

2._____

PLEASE ALLOW 4-6 WEEKS FOR SHIPPING

Submit Wholesale Orders to:
Kensington Publishing Corp.
C/O Penguin Group (USA) Inc.
Attention: Order Processing
405 Murray Hill Parkway
East Rutherford, NJ 07073-2316
Phone: 1-800-526-0275
Fax: 1-800-227-960